Catherine Fittler

IN HIS PLACE

by
Catherine Wittler

B & C Publishing

This book is a work of fiction. Any resemblance to actual persons, living or dead, is coincidental.

Catherine Wittler

Copyright © 1986 by Catherine C. Wittler

All rights reserved. No part of this book may be reproduced or transmitted in any form or by any means, electronic or mechanical, including photocopying, recording, or by any information storage and retrieval system, without permission in writing from the publisher.

ISBN 0-937239-00-3

Library of Congress 85-70241

Manufactured by Apollo Books, 107 Lafayette St., Winona, MN 55987

PRINTED IN THE UNITED STATES OF AMERICA

OTHER BOOKS BY THE AUTHOR:

Novel
> *The Bungalow*

Poetry
> *Love*
> *Comfort*

Work and faith,
that's what it takes.
And one
without the other
is useless.

Dedication

To my wonderful husband, who has tolerated all the inconveniences of having a writer for a wife.
To my granddaughter, Maria, a fellow bookworm.

...C. W.

JACKET DESIGN BY DREW WITTLER

IN HIS PLACE

by

Catherine Wittler

CHAPTER 1

Since Ken Minard had left for his position in Pittsburgh a month earlier, Alexandria Ann Shaw had quarreled with everyone. Barry Lowe, her present companion, would not tolerate her selfish, obnoxious disposition, and had told her, in no uncertain terms, that he didn't want to see her again. Alex Ann stormed out of the club, snapping at everyone on the way, jumped into her car and sped off down the street.

"I'll show those opinionated snobs that I don't need any of them," she shouted aloud.

By the time she passed the third traffic signal, she was going well over the speed limit of forty. The city police immediately picked up her trail and sped after her.

Alex never slowed down. She just kept weaving in and out of traffic. By the time she reached the intersection of I-4, she was going eighty miles an hour. The police car tried to take due caution, but was held up by traffic coming off the side streets.

Alex raced up the runway to I-4 and out onto the highway without looking to the left or right. Suddenly, a Yield sign loomed up in front of her. She slammed on the brakes, but it was too late.

A semitrailer truck, coming up the highway, tried to swerve into the left traffic lane to avoid the little red Mercedes, but he didn't make it. The front end of the truck hit the car and flipped it over three times. It came to rest on the edge of an embankment. The truck driver braked as quickly as possible, jumped out of the truck and ran back to the car. He stood helplessly by, not quite knowing what to do. By that time, the police had arrived. They got out of the car and joined the driver.

"What's that crazy broad trying to do?" the driver stormed. "Kill herself?"

"Looks that way," one of the officers replied, as she approached the car to see if there was anything that could be done. "Let's get her out of here," he directed. "Radio for an ambulance!" he instructed his partner.

Officer Cameron ran to the police car and reported the accident, then called for an ambulance. He then hurried back to the scene and helped the other two men lift the unconscious woman from the wreckage and carry her as far away as possible, in case the car blew up or caught on fire.

"She's hurt badly, but she's alive," the first officer noted. "Wonder who she was running from. Cam, see if you can find a handbag and identify her."

Officer Cameron returned to the car, searched for a few minutes and came up with her billfold. He whistled as he extracted an ID card.

"Guess who?" he questioned, with raised eyebrows.

"Who is she? Anyone we know?" the other officer asked.

"She's Senator Sam Shaw's daughter," Cameron announced. "They live in that lavish house on the bay. I'll call in and have the clerk notify her parents."

"She's their only child, too," Officer Murphy sighed.

"Rich kids!" Cameron snorted. "They'll do it every time. Someone must have disappointed her." He shook his head as he studied the wreckage. "The car is a total loss, too. They'll never be able to fix that wreck."

Within the next few minutes, the ambulance sped up to the scene, sirens screaming. The emergency crew did a quick examination of Alex, loaded her into the vehicle and hurried on their way.

"N...now what?" the stunned truck driver stammered. "Man, that really threw me. I couldn't have gotten out of her way for anything. She drove right in front of me."

"We understand," Murphy nodded. "It wasn't your fault, but I still have to write up the accident before we can release you."

"Yeah, sure," the driver nodded.

The ambulance backed into the emergency entrance of the hospital and hurried Alex into a nearby examining room.

"Has her next of kin been notified?" questioned the resident on duty.

"Yes," Officer Murphy nodded. "She is the daughter of Senator Sam Shaw. They have been called and will be here shortly. She's all yours unless there's something more we can do."

"I guess not. You've done your part. You know, I marvel every time I'm on emergency duty at the terrible waste," the resident said, shaking his head sadly. "Why do people like this think they have to kill themselves or attempt to? Do they realize all the trouble and sorrow they cause?"

Officer Murphy motioned to his partner. "Let's wait in the emergency waiting room until the parents arrive," he suggested. "Maybe they can tell us why she did this."

"She usually drives a white convertible," Cameron noted. "I thought her father traded in that Mercedes."

Sam and Mervice Shaw ran up the ramp and entered the emergency waiting room and were confronted by the two young officers.

"We are the Shaws," Sam explained. "We were told that our daughter has been brought here."

"I'm Officer Murphy and this is Officer Cameron," one of the policemen said. "We were at the scene of the accident. In fact, we were pursuing your daughter because she was speeding. We didn't catch her in time, and she sped right into the path of a truck. Her car was demolished and she was seriously injured."

"Alexandria?" Mervice Shaw asked anxiously. "Is she really hurt badly?"

"Yes, ma'am, she is," Officer Murphy nodded.

At that moment, the double doors to the examining room sprung open and a young resident came toward the group.

"How is she, doctor?" Sam asked frantically, barely able to control the emotions that threatened to surface at any moment.

"She's in very serious condition," the resident answered truthfully. "I'm having her moved to fourth floor, where an orthopedic man and someone from neurology can examine her. I'm afraid she has a broken back."

"Oh, no!" Mervice cried. "Will she live? Will she be all right?"

"There's no way of telling at this time. We'll have to wait and see what they say on the fourth floor. If you wish to wait up there, there is a solarium at the end of the hall. I'll inform them of where you are," he explained. "Now, if you'll excuse me, time is of the essence right now." The young man turned abruptly and went back through the double doors through which he'd come moments before.

"Oh, Sam!" Mervice cried. "What shall we do? Our baby! What shall we do?" Mervice was near hysteria.

"Try to be calm," Sam soothed ineffectually. "Alex needs us now, as she's never needed us before. If only Ken were here," he muttered dejectedly. "We've got to tell him!"

"Why?" Mervice demanded. He isn't interested in her. He doesn't care about Alexandria. He went away and left her, didn't he?"

"Come on, darling," Sam urged. "Let's go upstairs where we'll be close by if there is any news, and let's pray very hard, for that's all that will help now." Sam Shaw put his arm around his wife and led her to the elevator.

After Ken Minard made rounds at the hospital that morning, he went to both local newspapers and put ads in the classified columns for a medical secretary, with experience, and an office technician.

When he returned to the office, there was an urgent message for him to call Tampa, Florida. Ken recognized the number right away. He immediately realized that something must have happened to Alex Ann.

No, he mused, *she would never allow them to call me. She hasn't even written since I left.*

He picked up the telephone, dialed direct, and was greeted by Sam Shaw's voice at the other end.

"What's wrong, Sam?" Ken asked. "How can I help?"

"It's Alexandria," Sam replied. "She's been in a car accident. She needs surgery, and the hospital here says they aren't equipped to perform the kind of operation she needs. I want to bring her to Pittsburgh, where you can look after her."

"But I'm not a surgeon, Sam," Ken protested. "Why can't you take her to Gainesville? They have everything there at the medical center."

"Mervice and I feel we would rather have her where you could look in on her," Sam explained.

"What type of surgery does she need? What's wrong with her, Sam?" Ken asked.

"It's her back. They say she needs spinal surgery."

"Oh, dear God," Ken murmured. "Is her back broken?"

"Yes," Sam replied, his voice choking with emotion. "They're afraid she'll be paralyzed."

"Take it easy, Sam," Ken urged. "It might not be as bad as you think. Let's take it one step at a time. First, you can't bring her here by a commercial plane, because they won't take stretcher cases. Can you arrange to fly her here by private plane? I'll have an ambulance meet you at the airport," Ken suggested.

"Yes, I'll make all the arrangements as soon as the doctor says she can be moved," Sam promised.

"What about Alex?" Ken asked. "Will she agree to come?"

"We're not going to tell her," Sam answered simply. "We're just telling her that we're moving her to another hospital."

"She won't stand for that. She's too inquisitive; she'll sense something is wrong right away," Ken cautioned.

"I don't think so," Sam countered. "She's so depressed, she's lost her will to live, it seems. I thought that if she knew you cared enough to want to help her, she would try harder."

"Sam, this will be a tremendous shock when she finds out where she is," Ken declared. "Aren't you afraid of the risk involved?"

"I'm afraid not to," Sam admitted. "Her mother and I feel that this is the only answer, medically and psychologically. We have to try, Ken. We're at our wits' end. I'm sure Mervice and I can reason with Alex when we are there and she finds there is some hope for her."

"All right, Sam," Ken finally agreed. "I'll do all I can, and I'll have everything ready when you arrive. I'll find the best neurosurgeon in Pittsburgh and engage his services. Are you prepared for the expense?" Ken asked.

"Alexandria is our only child," Sam replied. "We'll spend every cent we have if it will help her to walk again."

"Okay, call me as soon as you're ready. If it's at all possible, we'll have her walking again," Ken promised. Ken wanted to give Sam some encouragement, even though it might be unfounded.

After he'd hung up, Ken had second thoughts. *What if it's impossible to help Alex?* he wondered. *What if she's paralyzed for life? She wouldn't be able to cope with that.*

Ken Minard spent part of that afternoon thinking about Alexandria Shaw, how he'd met her and how they came to be parted. It had all started with a visit to his old friend, Dr. John Blanding, who had been almost like a father to him through the years.

It had been a smooth trip, except for a slight turbulence when they left the Tampa airport. The sun shone the rest of the way, and the view from the window seat of the big jet was like a toy city. Houses were nestled in and out of the hills of Virginia and Pennsylvania.

"We are now approaching the Pittsburgh Airport," the stewardess announced.

It had been a long time since Ken Minard had been to Pittsburgh. He glanced around to see how many other passengers were preparing to deplane at the airport. There were a dozen or more gathering together magazines and belongings.

"How long will it be before we land?" Ken asked the stewardess.

"About twenty minutes," the strikingly beautiful girl replied.

"Good, then I'll have time to freshen up," Ken decided out loud.

Ken Minard was six feet two inches tall, with raven black wavy hair and dark, brown skin, which was a result of the intense Florida sunshine, rather than his race.

He had sleek, straight fingers and the narrow hands of a surgeon. His fingernails, always well manicured, were spotlessly clean. He gestured with his hands when he talked and they were naturally very obvious to the person listening. He was immaculate in his appearance; starched shirts, straight ties and perfectly pressed trousers. He moved with a quick, short step, and was to the back of the plane before he finished speaking.

When Ken finished freshening up, the plane was already circling the city. The beautiful hills of Pennsylvania covered with foliage of scarlet, burnt orange and brown were an incomparable sight, especially from the window of the jet, descending down, down, over the treetops to the vast runway below.

When the plane rolled to a stop, and all the passengers for the Pittsburgh station descended the steps of the plane, the brisk air of fall, and the sunny skies of an Indian Summer enveloped Ken.

He breathed deeply and thought, *Where in God's country is there anything to compare with this paradise?*

Ken looked longingly for a familiar face, but couldn't distinguish one in the hustle and bustle of the unloading and boarding of different planes going and coming from all parts of the country.

"Maybe my instructions were misunderstood," Ken thought aloud. *Then, perhaps, Dr. John's secretary forgot to make arrangements for my pickup,* he mused to himself. *I may have to take a cab,* he decided, as he walked toward the familiar terminal to pick up his luggage.

He hailed a taxicab and commanded, "Thirty-Second Street, please."

"Thirty-Second Street?" the driver repeated.

"That's right," Ken answered.

"You come to Pittsburgh often?" asked the driver when they'd driven a few blocks.

"Not very. It's been years since I've been here. Has it changed much? Thirty-Second Street, I mean."

"The whole city's changed," the driver admitted. "Where you from? California?"

"Florida," Ken corrected. "I used to live in Pittsburgh," Ken said reluctantly.

"What did you say your name was?"

"I didn't, but it's Minard"...Ken Minard."

"Oh!" the driver exclaimed knowingly. "You're the Senator! Senator Minard! You've been a big name in the news lately. You must know a lot of people from Florida. I once had an uncle who lived in Tallahassee. Hoover was his name. I don't suppose you knew him?"

"I'm afraid not," Ken replied. "Tallahassee is a large city and it's hard to get to know everyone. People are moving in and out every day. Some come, like it, and stay. Others come and are disillusioned. Before long, they return to the environment where they grew up."

The driver swung around the corners and through traffic expertly. Undoubtedly, he'd been a taxi driver here most of his adult life. Ken, peering out the window, had forgotten how narrow the streets were and how close together the houses were. Town houses were built in row after row, all with the same floor plan. They were two-storied, with the living quarters downstairs and the bedroom upstairs. Some were even three stories.

Pittsburgh was one of the dirtiest cities in the United States. It had changed very little. Heavy industry, steel mills and smoke from coal-fired furnaces had made it that way. It was no exception now; the curbs were lined with dirt. It seemed to Ken the streets were never cleaned. Maybe it only appeared this way because Florida cities were cleaner, the streets were wider and the houses were not boxed so close together.

The taxi stopped in front of Dr. John Blanding's house on Thirty-Second Street a short time later. Leaves of the big elm and maple trees had begun to fall, and they blanketed the lawn that would not need to be mowed until spring. Rustling leaves brought back memories to Ken, for the trees in Florida did not shed all their leaves.

As he and Dr. Blanding walked up the concrete sidewalk to the front porch, the doctor said very apologetically, "I'm sorry I didn't meet you at the airport, my boy, but I had a few last minute calls, and then my secretary is not always on the ball. She didn't cancel out my appointments early enough. Nevertheless, you're here, and that's the important thing." He shook Ken's hand and slapped him twice on the back, as he steered him toward the front door.

"Think nothing of it," Ken replied. "I enjoyed the cab ride and the conversation with the driver. Pittsburgh has changed, but then I guess all cities do from decade to decade."

"Just park your bags there in the hallway," the doctor directed, "and follow me into the dining room. I'll bet you haven't had any dinner and are practically starved."

"You're right," Ken grinned. "I was in such a rush to make my plane that I didn't take time to eat lunch. They served a light lunch on the plane, but it didn't fill me up," he admitted.

It was seven p.m., and Ken was a lot hungrier than he let on. He desperately wished for a steaming cup of coffee. That was all he could concentrate on when he entered the dining room and got a sniff of the coffee aroma coming from the kitchen.

Quinter, the waiter and handyman who had worked for Dr. Blanding for years, sensed Ken's dilemma and remarked, "How nice to see you again, Dr. Minard." The two shook hands. "You are undoubtedly famished. How would it be if I just bring you the whole pot of coffee and you can help yourself to whatever you want?"

"That's the best offer I've had today," Ken said thankfully.

"After we've eaten, Quinter will show you to your quarters, unpack your bags and prepare your bath, if you like," the doctor stated.

"Oh, that won't be necessary," Ken protested. "Just show me where I'm to sleep, and I can do the rest myself. I can't afford to let you spoil me like that."

Ken would have welcomed the attention, but didn't want to get off on the wrong foot with the doctor on his first evening there.

"I don't think you'll have any choice. Quinter will insist. Why not let him indulge himself? He doesn't have the privilege of serving a Senator every day." Dr. Blanding smiled.

"Well!" Ken exclaimed. "We can't disappoint Quinter, can we?"

The bedroom that Ken was to use during his stay with Dr. Blanding was a spacious one, as were all the rooms in the house. There was a king-sized bed, with a huge, foam mattress and pillows to match. A night commode stood beside the bed, with an elegant lamp and a telephone at his disposal. The matching dresser and chest were Italian period furniture—vast, heavy and very masculine. There was ample room in the wardrobe for all the changes of clothing that Ken had brought with him.

Since the bedroom was on the third floor, and the Blanding home sat on a hill overlooking the city, the view from his window was far and wide. Since it was dusk, or twilight, as it is referred to in Western Pennsylvania, Ken could see block after block of the city. Lights blinked on and off, and store windows lit up in the department stores housing all the latest styles of winter fashions, something that Floridians seldom wore.

He stood and looked out the window for what seemed to be hours, but could have been only seconds.

"Your bath is ready, Senator," Quinter announced. "If there's anything else I can help you with, just ring this bell." He pointed to the bedside commode. "Feel free to retire whenever you like. Have a splendid night's rest."

All the attention was overwhelming to Ken, but why not enjoy it while he could? He prepared for bed and, before dropping off to sleep, his mind wandered back to earlier years when he'd lived in Pittsburgh.

Ken Minard had been born in a rather poor section of Pittsburgh. His father was a steel worker, and his mother died when he was a boy. Ken was raised by his father as well as the help of Dr. and Mrs. John Blanding, who had no children. They looked upon Ken as an adopted son, and to Ken were like another set of parents.

Ken always wanted to be a doctor. When he finished high school, he went to medical school in Philadelphia, then came back to Pittsburgh to take his internship and residency, because he could be near his father and work with Dr. Blanding.

After his residency, he joined the armed forces and became a captain in the Medical Corps. During the three-year hitch, his father died, and when Ken was discharged, he settled in Tampa, Florida. He went into practice with a team of doctors at the Ressler Clinic for Internal Medicine. Through his practice at the clinic, Ken met Sam Shaw, a Florida State Senator.

Sam was a politician—a good one. His physical problem was not serious, but each time he came to Dr. Ken Minard's office, he brought up the subject of politics. Ken had complained to Sam about some of the out-of-date medical laws in Florida, and because of this, he felt that Ken was the perfect candidate for the running mate on the ballot that fall.

"I think you should run for the Senate on the ticket this fall," Sam announced.

"I'm no politician!" Ken protested. "I'm a doctor! I don't know the first thing about politics."

"That's what others say until they get involved and find they know more than they think they do." Sam replied. "You're just the kind of man we need in the Senate. You have a good medical background, and we need some new laws in this state regarding medical practices. You said so yourself. You might be the man to push them through."

First and foremost, Ken was a doctor. It was his greatest love. However, Sam Shaw was just as good a politician and very persuasive.

"I've studied hard, spent thousands of dollars to become a doctor," Ken argued, "and I can't chuck it all by walking away from my patients and into a field I'm not even familiar with."

Sam Shaw didn't give up. On the ballot that fall, after intense electioneering, Ken Minard's name appeared on the ticket. He was elected, and the next three years were a long, hard struggle. During that time, Ken often wondered why he'd let Sam talk him into such a demanding profession.

He had served his term; he had been a good statesman, but it was time, once again, for his name to come up. Did he want to be a Senator again? He missed medicine and was not as enthused about politics as Sam had led him to believe he would be.

Fate had perhaps called again for Ken to go back to his first love. When the call came from Dr. Blanding, Ken had responded almost automatically, and agreed to the visit. In the morning, he would learn why his old friend had invited him.

Dr. Blanding had been a friend of the Minard family for many years. He was there when Ken's mother passed away. She had suffered long and hard from a malignancy for which there was no cure or hope. Ken was only ten years old when Luticia Minard died.

He was an only child, and the loss of his mother, whom he adored, was a cruel burden for Ken to bear. During the next few years, he turned instinctively to Dr. Blanding's wife for the motherly attention he needed. His father never remarried, and when Ken was drafted into the armed forces during the Korean War, he was stationed in Florida. His father died while Ken was serving in Korea, so naturally when Ken returned and was discharged, he settled in Tampa Bay in Florida.

For some reason, Ken didn't feel ready to return to Pittsburgh, with its sad memories of his youth. Until he heard from Dr. Blanding, Ken had heard nothing of his hometown.

CHAPTER 2

At breakfast the following morning, Ken waited patiently for Dr. Blanding to reveal his reason for summoning the young man to his home. The answer was not long in coming.

"I need someone to take over my practice, Ken," Dr. Blanding announced. "I'm not as young as I used to be and these winters in Pittsburgh get colder every year."

"Ah! Don't kid me, doc," Ken grinned. "You have lots of years left for practicing medicine. You're one of the best, and you've always loved Pittsburgh."

"Maybe so," the doctor noted thoughtfully, "but I doubt if I'll be here next year. You see, Ken, I have cancer, and I have only a short time to live. One year, or two, who knows? I want you to come into practice with me. I want to teach you all I can in the short time I have left, then you will take over my practice," Dr. Blanding explained.

Ken was astonished beyond words. It couldn't be—not Dr. Blanding. He wasn't that old, and he was needed so badly. Still, cancer was no respecter of persons, and Dr. Blanding was just as susceptible as the next person. Even so, what did one say to someone as dear as the doctor was to Ken? How could he soften the blow he'd just received?

"Are you sure your case is fatal?" Ken finally asked. "Have you been to more than one doctor for other opinions? Maybe the doctors here are wrong."

"It's no use, Ken; I've been everywhere," Dr. John admitted. "They all say the same thing." Suddenly he added,

"You can live right here with me; this house is big enough for both of us, and when I'm gone you'll be here to continue on. We could convert more of the first floor into office space if you want."

"But...Dr. John, I've been out of touch for four years. Politics took all my time. I'm not up on the latest aspects of medicine," Ken protested.

"I realize that," Dr. John nodded. "That's why I asked you to come here now and work with me. Pittsburgh has just about everything that the medical profession has to offer. My only regret is that I must leave this earth with so much yet undone," he said sadly.

Ken's heart ached, although he knew this was typical of the medical world. Some patients could be helped, but others were beyond anything human knowledge could conjure up. God was their only help.

"Look, Dr. John, will the people want to come to a new doctor after having you as their savior for so many years?" Ken asked. "Will they want a young 'whippersnapper' like me? Will they trust my judgment?"

"Yes, they'll flock to you like sheep to the fold," his friend nodded. "Every young woman and girl who learns there is a virile, handsome, young doctor in my office will be camping in the waiting room. It'll be up to you to keep them as patients or dismiss them as you see fit."

You make it sound so easy," Ken said uneasily. "The opportunity is such that I would be a fool to turn it down."

Ken thought of sunny Florida, the differences in the climate, and the overall environment. How could he leave all that for smoky, dirty, cold and windy Pittsburgh? Still, Ken had studied in Philadelphia at the University of Pennsylvania School of

Medicine, and had even taken some courses in Germany, one of the coldest countries in the world as far as he was concerned.

"Oh, I'm sorry, Ken; I forgot to ask," Dr. John said. "Are you married?"

"No," Ken replied. "I've never found the right girl, I guess. I do have a girl friend, but I'm sure she wouldn't fit into my position here, but I'm not certain it would be that important. That's not my problem. Before I decide on something this severe, I would have to think about it carefully."

"Suppose you do that," Dr. John agreed. "In the meantime, while you're here, follow me around for a day or two and see if there's anything at all that could persuade you to take the position," he suggested.

"You have a deal," Ken smiled. "I don't need to be back in Tampa until Friday. We can cover a lot of territory in three days, doc, so let's begin whenever you're ready."

Ken was trying to be as cheerful as possible, since he knew this great man was suffering from a hopeless malady. However, Ken felt Dr. John's shoes far too big for him to step into.

"The first thing on the agenda is the hospital," Dr. John announced. "I make rounds first thing every morning, then see patients from ten to twelve. I eat lunch if I have time, then see more patients from two to four. I like to make evening rounds again, but don't always have time to do everything I would like. With complaining old ladies, frightened children and all kinds of emergencies, we get tied up, and are sometimes here until six in the evening."

Dr. John had patients in two, and often three, hospitals in the area. Thus Ken Minard began his medical profession all over again by making rounds with Dr. John Blanding on that crisp, golden and orange morning. As they went from room to room, Ken was aware that he was being talked about.

"Oh, Brother, who's he?" he overheard one nurse exclaim.

"Somebody said Dr. Blanding was recruiting an associate. Isn't he a dream? Hope he takes the position," was the reply.

"He'll probably be one of those snooty know-it-alls who'll give us a hard time," the nurse decided.

"Honey, I'll take a chance on the hard time," the other person retorted. "Just give me the opportunity to work with him."

It went that way from day to day, until it was time for Ken Minard to return to Florida and his office as State Senator.

When he said good-bye to Dr. John, he thought, *How can I refuse this wonderful man a position such as he's offered me? Yet it's been so long since I've set a broken leg, seen a diseased gall bladder, or diagnosed a strep throat. Can I fall back into medical practice so quickly? It's a big order. Will I be able to fill it?*

On the plane, he wondered how he could leave all his friends and acquaintances. How easy would it be to close his beach home and walk away from it? However, doctors did get time off, and he could be back in Tampa in less than three hours. Every so often, he could have an associate to stand by, and spend a week or two on the beach. Then there were the holidays. Maybe things could be worked out.

His biggest problem finally struck him. Sam Shaw! What would he tell Sam? How could he convince Sam that politics had not been everything he's expected and that he had a wonderful offer to return to medicine?

The plane trip was so smooth and beautiful that, like Scarlett O'Hara, Ken thought, *I'll think about that tomorrow.*

He settled back in the seat to enjoy the restive ride and the drink the stewardess had just served him.

When Ken arrived at the Tampa airport, Alexandria Ann Shaw was there to meet him. He wondered how she'd found out about his flight plans. In all the fuss and commotion, Ken had completely forgotten about Alex Ann.

How would she feel if he left the political world, which was a demanding life, and re-enter medicine, which was even more demanding? As it was, she already complained that she never saw him, and medicine was practically an all-consuming profession. Now was certainly not the time to discuss it.

"Why didn't you tell me you were going away?" she demanded as he kissed her gently and held her close for a few seconds.

"I was on such a tight schedule that I had no time to call," he replied. "I needed to catch that 4:20 flight from Tampa, and just couldn't stop to phone anyone."

"You could have called after you arrived," she accused. "Sometimes I think you don't care anything about me at all."

"Yes, I'm guilty. I should have called, but I was terribly busy."

Ken felt a bit sheepish about not calling Alex Ann, but he didn't want her to know where he'd gone. Not just then, anyway. He was quite sure she wouldn't approve of his trip or anything that would take him away from the political world.

Alex Ann was the only daughter of Sam Shaw, and because her father had been instrumental in persuading Ken to go into politics, she felt she had some claim on him.

Ken had met Alex Ann during the time he was treating her father for a stomach ulcer, and she invited Ken to their home for a meal at the first opportunity. Like all her other beaus, she latched onto him, and Ken soon found it impossible to say no to her. Ken, however, wasn't as enthused about their relationship as was Alex Ann. She had been raised in a political family, and

Ken was quite sure she could never fit into the life of a physician.

"I'm so glad you're home," Alex Ann bubbled. "Don't you go running off like that anymore without telling me. Promise?"

"I promise," Ken agreed shortly. "From now on you will be the first to know when I make a sudden trip, no matter where I go, okay? Is all forgiven?" Ken was becoming quite bored with Alex Ann's demands and smothering behavior.

"Only if you agree to have dinner with us this evening," she replied possessively. "We have a lot to discuss, and I know Father is anxious to hear about your trip, as am I."

Oh, boy, Ken thought. *Here goes. How am I going to tell the Shaws that I have been offered a position in medicine in, of all places, Pittsburgh, Pennsylvania?*

"It's been a long three days, Alex Ann, and I'm a bit tired," Ken countered. "Couldn't we postpone the dinner until tomorrow evening?"

"Never!" Alex Ann exclaimed belligerently. "I won't hear of it. Surely you can spend your first evening back with me."

"All right," Ken agreed wearily. "Drop me off at my place and let me freshen up. I'll be at your house at seven tonight." At that point, Ken's only interest was in keeping peace.

Alex Ann left Ken at his spacious beachfront home, and after kissing him lightly said, "Now, remember, seven o'clock! Don't be late." Alex Ann's worst trait was her demanding personality. Everything went her way, or no way.

"I'll be there," he promised.

He then disappeared through the door, dropped his luggage and called to Loi, his houseboy, to unpack and put away his clothing while he showered and dressed for dinner at the Shaws. He would have liked it so much better to be able to settle into his big lounge chair in the den and watch the evening news and eat a sandwich.

If he dressed and showered quickly, and wasn't too particular about his appearance, he could relax in his favorite chair for about thirty minutes. That would be long enough to permit his heart to slow down and his blood pressure to drop to a more normal stage.

The big, black lounge chair in the corner of his den, where the walls were lined with medical books, gave Ken an excellent view of the garden outside. The grass was always so green and so delicately manicured.

During the rainy season in Florida, the grass needed to be mowed at least once a week, and sometimes twice. In the fall, it didn't grow as fast. Rain was not as frequent and lawns had to be watered daily to keep them as beautiful as was Dr. Ken Minard's. Loi, an all-around handyman, saw to that.

Ken's mind wandered far from the beautiful lawn and spotless glass doors and windows in his den. He had just had an offer to return to his first love—medicine.

He worried the most about what Alex Ann would say. She was somewhat of a snob, but it wasn't entirely her fault. Mervice Shaw, her mother, was not the athletic type, but she belonged to all the best clubs and social organizations in Tampa. She was trying desperately to draft Alex Ann into the same way of life. Alex had been taught to attend only the best concerts, ballets and social parties given by the high society of the area.

Alex Ann, however, wasn't too keen on following in her mother's footsteps. She wasn't the type to be tied down to times and places. She hated bridge, although her mother was a successful bridge champion and chided Alex Ann for not taking more interest in the game.

When Alexandria Ann Shaw turned twenty-one, her father thought she should become more involved in politics.

"Oh, Daddy! Politics are for men!" she protested. "Woman just sit on the sidelines, give parties and cheer their favorite man into office."

"That's not so, Alexandria," her father protested. "Times have changed. Women are taking more interest in politics and I think you should begin to do just that."

"You're just mad because I'm a girl and you never got your precious son to follow in your footsteps," she shouted.

That was partially true. Sam Shaw was disappointed that he'd never had a son, and perhaps Ken Minard was the substitution for the son he'd never had.

"Alexandria, sometimes you can be a highly impossible child, a trait acquired from your mother. I wish you would learn to be a little more discreet and hold your temper."

Alex Ann stomped off, ignoring her father's last remark.

Ken Minard was aware of all these things, and wondered how he would begin to tell the Shaw family of his offer, and what their reaction would be if he accepted.

The thirty minutes passed so quickly, then Ken had to dash to his bedroom, dress hurriedly in order to be at the Shaws in time for his seven o'clock appointment.

The excellent food served was the one thing Ken could depend on when he went to the Shaw home. Since Mrs. Shaw was either too busy or too sophisticated to cook, a full-time cook was employed, as was a maid and gardener-handyman.

On the Gulf coast of Florida, seafood was in abundance, and Vera, the Shaw's cook, could bake fish that smelled delicious and melted in one's mouth. She was very reluctant to pass on her numerous recipes to just anyone, but Ken felt that if he ever got married, Vera could be persuaded to give his new wife a few of her recipes.

Mrs. Shaw answered the door, and Ken gave her the usual hug and slight brush of a kiss to her cheek.

"I'm glad you accepted Alex Ann's invitation to have dinner with us," she greeted Ken. "She says you've been away for a few days. Come in and tell us all about your trip," she urged.

Oh brother! Ken thought unhappily. *How do I get myself into such situations? Why couldn't I have been a plumber or a convict or something less complicated?* He knew there would be no way of getting around Mervice Shaw's persistent questions.

He knew a cute little nurse he'd met at the hospital, while he was still practicing, and having dinner with Judy would have been so much more simple. There would be no questions or accusations—just quiet talk, a goodnight kiss and peace of mind. How could he have been so dumb as to get involved in politics?

Dinner was a long, drawn out process. It was served in courses, and each time, Mervice Shaw had some correction or addition to the service.

As time slipped by, Ken began to think he might be able to escape early and not have to answer the inevitable questions.

Just as he began to relax, Alex remarked, "Ken Minard, how dare you go off somewhere for a whole week and not tell us where you're going or when you'll be back?"

"I explained that once, Alex," Ken replied stiltedly. "I didn't have much time. I was just called away suddenly."

"Well, now you can tell us, can't you?" she quipped."

"Yes, now I'll try to explain where I went and why," Ken nodded. "However, I'm not sure what the outcome will be, for I haven't decided on that yet." Ken took a deep breath, then began in a calm voice. "I received a phone call from a Dr. John

Blanding of Pittsburgh, asking if I could fly up to Pennsylvania and visit with him for a few days. He sounded almost desperate, so I left at once."

"Without even asking him why!" Alex Ann exclaimed. "That seems rather unusual."

"Keep quiet, Alexandria," Sam retorted. "Let Ken finish."

"Dr. Blanding has been a friend of my family for many years," Ken explained. "He was with us when my mother died. I was only a boy then, and we've kept in touch ever since. He knew that I had gone into politics and wasn't sure if I'd be interested in his proposition."

"What proposition, Ken?" Sam asked, apparently getting an uneasy feeling as the conversation progressed.

"He wants me to come to Pittsburgh and go into practice with him, so I will be able to continue his mission in life after he's gone," Ken announced. "You see, he has terminal cancer and has only a short time to live."

"How terrible," remarked Mervice, with a slight shake of her head. "Does he have a family, or anyone, who can look after him?"

"No, Ma'am, he has no one," Ken replied, "but he's not worried about himself. His practice is his only concern. This is the only way I can help him."

"You wouldn't!" Alex Ann almost shouted. "You surely wouldn't do such a thing! How can you even think about it?" she demanded, almost hysterical. "You wouldn't dare leave Tampa, your profession as a statesman and me! Ken Minard, how could you?"

"Alex Ann, try to calm yourself," Ken answered wearily. "I haven't decided anything. I've been out of medicine for four years, and I'm not sure I could pick it up and go on as before. I'd have a lot of studying to do to catch up. It would mean a great deal of work before I even began practicing again. However, I have to make a decision shortly. Dr. Blanding doesn't have long to live, and I'd need all the help he could give me in the short time he has left. If I decide to go, I'd have to leave almost immediately."

"You've been a good Senator, Ken," Sam admitted. "You could go on to be a better one, of that I'm sure. However, a man must do what he must do. If you feel that going to Pittsburgh and working with Dr. Blanding is your goal in life, then that's what you must do. We must be careful not to interfere or dissuade you wrongly in any way." He looked at Alexandria with a stern expression on his face. "None of us," he added.

"Thank you, Sam," Ken said, quite relieved. "It takes a great person and a God-fearing man to admit what you just did. I respect you highly for your faith and confidence in me."

"Well, I think you're all crazy!" Alex Ann shouted. "Why can't we go on as we are? Why do you have to be a doctor and see all those sick people and go to all those smelly old hospitals? What about your house here? What about me, Ken? What about me?"

"Alex Ann, I'm not leaving tomorrow," Ken sighed. "We will discuss these things later and work them all out, if I decide to accept the position in Pittsburgh."

"I think we've talked enough now," Mervice interjected. "Let's let it rest and enjoy our dessert and talk of pleasanter things. We can discuss all of this another time. Ken is undoubtedly tired and would like to go home and get a good night's rest."

Alex Ann said no more; neither did she eat her dessert. When Ken left to go home, she was exceptionally cool to him.

"Will I see you tomorrow?" Ken asked.

"If you're sure you want to be bothered with a mere Senator's daughter," Alex retorted snobbishly.

"You know I do. We'll talk about all this later. Good night, Alex Ann."

Ken drove home quickly, parked his car in the garage, went into the house to his bedroom, undressed and dropped into bed, completely exhausted. In minutes, he was asleep.

Alex Ann didn't give up so easily. She continued to rant and rave after Ken left.

"How could he do such a thing? I hate him! I hate him for being so cruel!"

"Go to bed, Alexandria," Sam commanded shortly, "and stop jumping to conclusions. This will all work out all right."

Mervice Shaw, however, wasn't so sure, although she said nothing. She knew Ken Minard, and he had a mind of his own. He would do what he thought best, no matter how much pressure was imposed upon him.

Alex Ann went to her room, but she took an hour to undress.

Ken surely wouldn't do such a crazy thing, she thought. *Why would any handsome young man, with everything going for him, chuck it all and move to a smelly, old town like Pittsburgh? And all our friends—what will they say?*

Alex slipped into a maize-colored gown and sat on the edge of her beautiful canopied bed. The canopy, spread and frilly curtains all matched. They were yellow, like the gown she wore, mainly because it was her favorite color. However, her mother was the "Queen Bee," and Alex's room was more Mervice's idea than it was her daughter's.

Alex Ann couldn't be bothered with such trivia; she was too busy flirting with all the boys in her social class. Her great aim in life was to marry a handsome young man with lots of money. Even though Ken Minard wasn't yet rich, there was every possibility that he would make a fortune if he played it right. If he ran off to Pittsburgh, though, to practice medicine with some stuffy old doctor, he would be buried forever.

Alex could not allow that to happen, but how was she going to prevent it? She scooted into bed and turned off the light, thinking, *Tomorrow I'll try a new strategy. I've got to keep Ken here in Florida, with me. Mother and I will think of something.*

CHAPTER 3

Ken jumped out of bed at seven a.m. the next morning, and made ready to get to his office by eight-thirty. It didn't give him much time. After he shaved, ate his breakfast of eggs and orange juice—the juice squeezed from the oranges grown on the trees in his back yard—and had his usual two cups of coffee, he would be able to make it as far as the little coffee house near his office. It was there that all the professional men stopped for their last cup of coffee or tea before starting the working day.

He especially wanted to talk with a couple of his lawyer friends and discuss the proposition Dr. Blanding had offered him. Since his term of office would not be up until mid-January, he had plenty of time to seek advice from many of his colleagues and associates.

Joe Darby was at Ben's Grill when he arrived, and he immediately struck up a conversation with Ken.

"Where have you been?" Joe asked. "I haven't seen you all week. Someone said you flew to Pittsburgh. What business could you possibly have in Pittsburgh this time of year?"

"That's what I wanted to talk to you about," Ken replied. "My term of office ends in mid-January, and I have an offer to go back into medicine with a Dr. Blanding, an old friend of my family. What do you think of my giving up the Senate race and accepting the position?" Ken held his breath until Joe answered.

"Well, man, that's your choice. I don't see how anybody else can tell you what to do. However, I'd say you are very foolish if you throw away a promising political career and go back into a profession as demanding as medicine."

Joe Darby was a fortunate, young black attorney, associated with a large law firm. He felt he "had it made."

"Besides, what brought all this up so suddenly?" Joe questioned.

"Dr. Blanding is a very sick man; in fact, he has only a short time to live. He wants me to take over his practice in Pittsburgh and continue to serve his patients in the Blanding manner."

"What is the Blanding manner?" Joe inquired.

"Being available at all times," Ken answered simply. "He even makes house calls. That's unheard of in Florida for the most part. It's a big order. I've been out of medicine for four years, although I did keep up my medical magazines and sat in on a couple of lectures. I'm really rusty, though. That's why he wants me to come as soon as I can."

"What about your friends here, your position, your home? Ken, what about Alex Ann? How will she take this? And then there's Sam. What will he say?"

"Alex Ann is furious. She thinks I'm running out on her. She only considers herself and thinks as little as possible about others. Alex is a very spoiled and quite egotistical. As far as Sam is concerned, I really believe he would give me his blessing if he thought medicine was my real calling. I'm sure he realizes politics has not been all that I anticipated."

"Ken, this may be presumptuous of me, but how do you really feel about Alexandria?" Joe asked boldly. "Do you love her? Does she love you? Is it enough that she'd go with you as your wife?" Joe was beginning to realize what a complicated step this would be for Ken.

"Don't be silly, Joe," Ken grinned. "I'm fond of Alex Ann. I'm not sure I love her, but Alex Ann loves no one but herself.

She uses people as a means to her ends. She would never go with me to Pittsburgh. She couldn't bear to leave Florida, and all her highfaluting friends and yacht club members," Ken decided sadly.

"Will you ask her? I mean, if she cares enough to go with you?" Joe queried.

"Not now, Joe," Ken replied. "In the first place, I need to get established; that is, if I decide to go at all. I'll be living with Dr. Blanding, in his spacious home, but his offices are on the first floor, with living quarters on the second and third floors. I would need a housekeeper and maid for Alex, since she's been used to such treatment. I'm sure she'd never settle for less. It would be costly and I wouldn't have the means to handle such a drastic step at first.

"Then there's the weather," Ken continued. "It's cold in Pittsburgh in the winter, rainy in the spring and hot as blazes in the summer. It's smoggy and dirty from all the industry—truly not a very appetizing place to live, especially for someone like Alex."

"I'd say you're being confronted with quite a dilemma, Ken," Joe admitted. "I'm glad it's you that has to make the choice. I will say, though, that if you feel your calling is medicine, and this opportunity will open that field for you again, you'd be a fool not to consider it very earnestly."

"Thanks for listening, Joe," Ken said. "Now, I've got to get to my office and try to catch up on that inevitable backlog of work. See you tomorrow." Ken picked up his topcoat, slipped into it and was gone before Joe Darby had a chance to respond.

Sam Shaw had already left for his office when Alex Ann came down to breakfast. Her mother always slept late, but Alex Ann had to talk with her mother that morning.

When Alex passed her mother's bedroom, she poked in her head and called, "Mother, please get up and have breakfast with me. I want to talk to you."

"If it's about Ken Minard taking a position in another state, Alexandria, it's no use talking. He'll do just as he pleases no matter what you say."

"Don't say that, Mother," Alex groaned. "Please let's talk about it at breakfast. Just this once. Please, Mother," she begged.

Mervice was disgusted to be awakened before she was ready to get up, so she purposely took her time in dressing and preparing her makeup. She finally appeared in the elegant dining room.

She ate only toast and orange juice. She felt that coffee and tea were bad for her, and never indulged in either.

Alex wished that just once they could eat in the kitchen like normal people. It seemed so formal to have breakfast in the dining room, when she wanted to talk with her mother confidentially.

"Everything always takes you so long, Mother," Alex complained. "I'm all jitters waiting."

"Well, Alexandria, I'm not accustomed to being awakened so rudely and having someone demand my appearance at the breakfast table. You will have to mind your manners a little better in the future."

Manners, phooey! Alex thought. *I have more important things to do.*

"Mother," Alex began, "I'm worried about Ken. You don't think he would take that job with that stuffy old doctor in Pittsburgh, do you?"

"Well, that will have to be his decision," Mervice replied calmly. "I don't know what we could do about it."

"But we have to do something! I can't stand by and just let him walk out of my life," Alex whined.

"What if he asked you to go along?" Mervice suggested. "As his wife, I mean."

"You're not serious!" Alex shouted. "Go to that dirty old city of Pittsburgh, where it gets twenty below zero in the winter? Well, I never, Mother! You, of all people!"

"I only asked," Mervice replied, unruffled. "If you love Ken, though, you would go anywhere with him."

"Of course, I love him, but, Mother, I could never leave Tampa and you and Daddy and all my friends," Alex expostulated. "What would I do all day by myself while Ken was running around fixing broken bones and healing sore throats?"

"You could make new friends." Mervice was becoming quite bored with the conversation. "Lots of people move to other cities, make friends and are quite happy. Then, too, Alex, you might have a child and that would be wonderful company for you."

"Mother!" Alex exclaimed. "I just never! I've never heard you talk to foolishly. I knew you would be no help. Well, I'm going to talk to Daddy. He'll think of something. He has a lot of influence with Ken. He's just got to dissuade Ken from making such a fool of himself!" Alex's face showed a genuine worried expression. "I've got to run, Mother. I have a tennis match at ten-thirty, and I'm going to be late. I'll see you at lunch."

"Not today, darling," Mervice contradicted. "I have a luncheon at the Garden Club and the speaker is one I don't want to miss. I'll see you later in the day and we'll go over some of those patterns for your holiday formals."

Mervice Shaw was miserable because she could do nothing to help Alex Ann with her problem. Alex was such a flippity girl, going from one thing to another, but Mervice guessed it was partly her own fault. She was so involved herself and couldn't spend much time with either Sam or Alexandria. Maybe if she'd taken more time to teach Alexandria the values of life, she wouldn't have been so selfish and egotistical. Maybe if they'd had other children, and Alex would have had to share some of her love and affection with a brother, she would have had a nicer disposition.

Sam had always wanted a boy, but after Alex was born, Mervice felt that nothing was worth the misery of a nine-month pregnancy and a painful birth. Alexandria Ann Shaw got all the love, affection and attention of Sam and Mervice Shaw.

Perhaps it was too much attention expended in the wrong direction, and there was no real love and concern for her welfare. She had grown up to be a beautiful five-feet-seven-inch blonde. She didn't look like either of her parents, but rather a composite of both.

Mervice had blonde hair and fair, smooth-as-a-rose-petal complexion. Sam had a darker, more ruddy complexion. He was out-of-doors much of the time and had a beautiful, even Florida tan. Alex had her father's complexion and, since she water-skied and swam so much, she, too, had the even bikini tan of the native Floridians.

When Alex graduated from high school, her father gave her a brand new convertible. Just the previous year, when she turned twenty-one, he replaced it with a red and white sports car. Alex was always abusing her driving rights and her father warned her repeatedly that if she got stopped for speeding, or for any other offense, he wouldn't pay her fines. As far as he was concerned, she could sit in jail. Each time, he bailed her out.

It wasn't necessary for Alex to work after graduating from high school, and she fought her parents about going to college. However, they were able to persuade her to take some courses at the University of South Florida, so she could stay at home and commute daily. Much to their surprise, she passed with honors. Even though she was a college graduate, she still felt it was a waste of time except for the friends she had accumulated from her association there.

Thanksgiving and Christmas passed with the usual turkey, stuffing, gift-giving ritual of every year. Alex Ann and Ken attended the usual holiday parties, as did Alex's parents.

The New Year dawned much the same as other New Years, except for the fact that Ken had decided to take the position with Dr. Blanding. He put off telling Alex Ann of his final decision until after the holidays, purposely because he didn't want to spoil her good times.

However, the time had finally come when Ken needed to muster up all his courage and explain to Alex Ann that as soon as his term in the Senate ended, he would prepare to go to Pittsburgh and work with Dr. Blanding.

He decided to leave on the first of February, and when he was certain, he called Dr. Blanding and told his friend of his plans.

Dr. Blanding was elated. If Ken took over his practice, he could go on to a better world knowing his patients and friends were in good, responsible hands.

"I'll help all I can," the good doctor promised. "It will be a rigorous schedule, but if you are really conscientious, you'll withstand it. Only time will tell." Dr. Blanding breathed a silent prayer that he might be spared until this one last job on earth was completed.

New Years Eve was the big party, and Alex Ann looked more beautiful than ever.

It will be hard to leave Alex, Ken thought. *She is so beautiful and we have had some good times together.* He hoped that the evening would progress without the subject coming up, for if it did, he would be forced to explain.

His hopes were shattered when, after dancing the first three dances with Ken, Alex's next partner was the son of a friend of Sam Shaw's, Barry Lowe.

While dancing, Barry said, "I hear Ken is leaving for Pittsburgh to go back into medical practice."

"Who told you that?" she demanded hotly.

"I thought it was common knowledge. All the fellows are talking about it," Barry replied.

"There's not a word of truth in it," Alex protested. "It's true he was offered a position in Pittsburgh, but he'd be a fool to leave everything here and go to that disgusting place."

"Medicine is Ken's true profession," Barry objected. "I thought when he went into politics he was making a mistake."

"Well, if Ken wants to practice medicine so badly, he can do it right here in Tampa," Alex retorted. "There's no need for him to go traipsing off to some other place. This is his home. His friends are here."

"I'm sorry, Alexandria," Barry apologized, "I didn't mean to upset you."

On the way home from the party, Alex related to Ken her conversation with Barry Lowe.

"I told him it was a pack of lies, that if you wanted to practice medicine you could do it right here in Tampa where your friends are," she finished haughtily.

"I'm sorry to disappoint you, Alex," Ken began slowly. "I should have told you earlier, so you could hear it from me, rather than from some joker on the dance floor. It's true that I have accepted the position with Dr. Blanding, and I will be leaving the first part of February." Ken knew instantly that an explosion was about to descend upon him.

"Then I don't ever want to see you again!" Alex Ann forced between clenched teeth. "If you put your own feelings before mine and think your old medicine is more important, then go to Pittsburgh. Bury yourself in that smoky old place and never speak to me again!"

"I would ask you to come with me, but at this time I can't afford to have a wife to support. Things will be rough financially, for a while. After I get established and can provide a better atmosphere, will you marry me, Alex, and come to Pittsburgh to live?" Ken asked.

"Never! As far as I'm concerned, you're no longer a part of my life. I don't need you anymore!" Alex screamed. "I can go out with Barry Lowe any time I want."

"Then you really don't love me," Ken answered. "If you did, you would consider my point of view, or at least compromise a little."

"Love you?" she questioned. "Of course, I love you, but you have no right to ask me to do such a dumb thing."

Ken wondered if Alex really did know the meaning of love. She was so flippant and self-centered. He couldn't understand why he put up with her at all.

"I guess, then, this will be good-bye," he announced. "I was hoping to see you at least until it was time for me to leave in February."

When Ken stopped the car in front of her house, Alex jumped out, ran up the steps and slammed the door, not even bothering to comment on his last statement.

Ken's heart lurched. He drove home silently, deep in thought.

She'll change her mind and see me again, he decided. *What if she doesn't, though? What if I've lost her completely? Would it really be that important to me? I haven't dated many girls, but I've gone with Alex a long time—almost two years. It seems I always go back to her.*

Ken Minard lay awake a long time that night and thought about his future.

What a way to begin a New Year, he thought dejectedly.

CHAPTER 4

The first day of February dawned sunny and clear as most Florida February days. Ken had his Plymouth Fury packed to the hilt. Most of the space was taken up with a set of expensive medical books, a gift from the wife of a doctor friend of Ken's.

Dr. Wallace had died suddenly and Mrs. Wallace had no use for the books. She wanted someone to have them who would really appreciate them and Ken was the logical choice. It was better, she decided, to give them to some deserving medical colleague than to sell them to strangers.

Ken was appreciative of Mrs. Wallace's generous gift and was determined to take them with him, even though they took up a lot of space in the car. Somehow he managed to pack everything in that he needed. At least it would discourage him from picking up hitchhikers, for there was no place to sit.

Ken had mixed emotions that day. He was reluctant to leave everything and everybody he'd known and loved in Florida, but he was anxious to get moving and begin his new adventure in Pittsburgh.

His good-byes had all been said. Sam and Mervice Shaw hugged and kissed him and wished him well, making him promise he would drop down over a weekend now and then.

"Our home will always be open to you," Sam reassured Ken.

He gave Loi all the instructions he could think of and reminded him to call immediately if he had any difficulties.

Alex Ann refused to see Ken. She even refused to talk to him on the telephone.

"I have nothing to say to him," she explained haughtily. "He made his choice and it does not include me. Let him go. He'll live to regret it."

Her parents knew their daughter was making a decision she would regret the rest of her life, but nothing they said could change her mind.

Ken had calculated his mileage and decided that his first stop for the night would be somewhere in North or South Carolina. If he averaged five hundred and fifty miles per day, he could easily be in Pittsburgh in two days.

That is, if the weather holds, he thought grimly.

The trip was uneventful until he reached the southern part of North Carolina. It was raining there and the car radio was tuned to a weather station picking up a forecast from Richmond, Virginia.

"It is snowing now in Richmond and portions of the state north of here have already received as much as four inches of snow. Parts of Pennsylvania and New York have from eight to ten inches, and it's still snowing," the reporter announced.

Ken was not accustomed to driving in snow, and was slightly upset when he heard the forecast. If the weather got too bad, he would have to stop and stay at a motel until the roads were cleared. That would hold up his arrival, and he was very anxious to get to his destination.

He drove on, going up through the Shenandoah Valley of Virginia, he could enter the turnpike there. Surely, they would have the turnpike cleared because of the heavy truck traffic.

He stopped for gas and to have his oil and tires checked at a service station on Interstate 95. The attendants were all bundled up and it was blowing and snowing.

"If you have any sense at all, you'll find a motel room and not try to go any further this afternoon and evening," one of the men warned Ken.

"I'd like to get as far as the Pennsylvania Turnpike, if I can," Ken contemplated. "It should be cleared off for the heavy traffic."

"No way," the attendant replied. "All roads in central and western Pennsylvania are closed, and portions of the turnpike are impassable. Power lines are down and telephone service is out."

"I've got to get through at least by telephone to tell the folks that are expecting me that I'll be late," Ken protested.

"Where you headed?"

"Pittsburgh."

"Forget it," the young man answered. "They'll know you're stranded somewhere. Everyone else is."

"How long will it take to clear the highways so I can get through?" Ken questioned.

"Not more than a day, if the storm lets up and they can salt the highways."

"What do you mean, 'salt the highways?'" Ken asked. "Why would they do that? They used to put cinders on the roads when I lived here years ago."

"Salt melts the snow into slush and the trucks can plow it off twice as fast as they could with cinders," the man explained.

"Progress," Ken noted. "It's just everywhere. Isn't that hard on the under carriage of the vehicles?"

"No worse than cinders. You can hose off your car, if you've a mind to, after you arrive at your destination."

"Thanks a lot, fellow," Ken smiled. "This is sure a far cry from Tampa, Florida, where I just came from. It was eighty degrees the day I left, and it's hard to believe there is snow anywhere. Hard to imagine a person can get so cold all of a sudden. My fingers and feet are frozen!"

"You'll get used to it after you've been North for a while. It's not so bad as this all the time."

"Thank goodness for that," Ken replied. He got in his car and reluctantly drove on, hoping to find a motel with a good heating system where he could stop and relax until the crisis was over.

Two days later the weather forecast was a little more promising, and Ken resumed his trek to Pittsburgh. By taking the turnpike to the Irwin Interchange, he would miss most of the mountains, because they were tunnelled through, and it wasn't necessary to go over any of them. It was definitely a relief to Ken.

Dr. Blanding was astonished when he finally greeted Ken in front of his spacious home. He was wearing only a suit with a windbreaker overcoat; no gloves, boots or hat.

"No wonder you're frozen," he exclaimed. "You have to wear warm clothes here in the North."

"This was all I had," Ken explained. "I had hoped for milder weather, at least until I could manage to accumulate some heavier clothing."

"In February?" Dr. Blanding roared. "You really have forgotten how cold Pittsburgh can get! No worry, we'll have you outfitted in no time. Here, you can wear this sheepskin coat until we get the car unloaded. And, for heaven's sake, man, put on some gloves. Your hands are turning blue with the cold."

Dr. John began to think he'd taken on more than he'd bargained for. Ken Minard would adjust, hopefully, and it was only two months to spring. Rainy, muddy, cold spring. Maybe they would have an early one, making it a little easier for his Southern friend.

"Could we just unload the necessary things now and leave the rest until morning?" Ken asked. "I'm freezing!" His teeth chattered uncontrollably, and his gloved hands shook as he reached into the car for something to carry into the house.

"Have you anything that will freeze?" Dr. John asked. "Have you any antifreeze in your radiator?"

"Great day, am I rusty," Ken muttered. "I forgot all about antifreeze until I was in Virginia and the service station attendant mentioned it. I didn't do anything about it then, though. Will it freeze up?"

"Not in my garage," Dr. John announced. "It's heated. Let's just carry in these few belongings, and as soon as I move a few things to one side, you can drive into the garage. We can unload the rest of your books and gear later on, after you've warmed up and had something to eat."

Dr. Blanding tired easily. He noticed it more as the evening wore on. He was going to have to alter his schedule in order to stay active as long as possible.

"It took longer to drive up than I expected," Ken said. "I ran into a bad snowstorm in Virginia and had to stay in a motel for two nights and a day. The attendant at the service station suggested I hole up until the turnpike and freeways were opened, since I wasn't used to driving on icy roads. I welcomed the advice," Ken admitted.

"It won't take you long to get used to it after you've been here a few weeks," Dr. John reassured him. "Your blood will have to thicken up a little, though, so you don't feel like a warmed over ice cube." Dr. John was trying to be encouraging.

After Ken showered, shaved and dressed, in the same spacious room he's used on his first visit, he went down the stairs to join his friend for dinner.

Quinter was a prince of a manservant, and Ken knew the older man's heart was heavy at the thought of losing Dr. Blanding.

"We have a lot to talk about, a lot of plans to make and only a short time in which to accomplish it all," Dr. John said. "Welcome to my home and my practice, Ken. I appreciate, beyond words, your accepting my proposition."

"I only hope I can be half as good as you anticipate," Ken replied, more sure than ever that the task ahead would be practically insurmountable.

As they were finishing their dessert, the telephone rang. Quinter answered it.

"It's for you, Dr. John. It's a Mrs. Moore. She said little Alice is worse. Could you come right away?" Quinter related.

"Tell her I'm on my way," Dr. John instructed.

"You're going out this time of night?" Ken asked.

"Of course," Dr. John retorted. "These people need me, and I would never forgive myself if anything happened to that little child."

"Let me go with you," Ken begged.

"That's not necessary. It's your first night here and you need to get organized."

"I'll get organized tomorrow," Ken protested. "Please, sir, I'd like to accompany you."

"Then get into a warm coat from the rack in the hall, and put on some overshoes. No need to get your feet wet and come down with a cold the first week you're here," Dr. John decided.

As they drove to the Moore home, Ken questioned Dr. John about Alice Moore.

"She has a bad case of influenza and she's not a strong child to begin with. I'm afraid she'll develop pneumonia. If her temperature is up again, I'm going to insist they put her in the hospital. It'll be hard to convince them, but I'm going to persuade them that she will get well faster."

Alice Moore was twelve years old, and a delicate child, small for her age. Ken could see as soon as they approached her bedside that she was struggling to breathe.

Dr. Blanding introduced Ken to the Moore family, then went to examine little Alice. The doctor was reasonably sure she had pneumonia, but he wanted to have her X-rayed to confirm his diagnosis. He suggested that they take her to Children's Hospital.

"Will it hurt?" Alice asked, frightened. "I don't want to go to the hospital. Can Mama stay with me?"

"Of course, your mama can stay with you," Dr. John reassured the child, "until you go to sleep. Then there will be lots of nurses to look after you until your mama returns the next day."

He turned to speak with Alice's parents. "Bundle her up in a wool blanket," he instructed. "I'll take her in my car and enter her right from the emergency room. You, George, can follow in your car. Mrs. Moore can ride with Alice and Dr. Minard in my car."

Clarice Moore wrapped Alice in a wool blanket right over her pajamas, and slipped fuzzy woolen slippers on her tiny feet.

"I want him to carry me," Alice announced as they prepared to leave, pointing to Dr. Ken Minard. "He's prettier."

"Anything you say, young lady," Ken agreed, picking up the fragile little girl and proceeding to the car.

He desposited her on the back seat of the car, with her head on her mother's lap, and in that instant Ken knew he had returned to his real calling, the healing of the sick.

How could I ever have given up medicine for politics? he wondered as they sped to the hospital. *It's taken a little twelve-year-old angel to bring me back to reality.*

Alice Moore was entered into the hospital and instructions given for medication. After Dr. John assured the Moores that Alice would be all right, barring complications, he and Dr. Minard drove home to Thirty-Second Street and a warm cozy fireplace. Another medical crisis had passed. Neither knew, however, how many more there would be that night.

After being with Dr. Blanding for almost a month, Ken discovered that his friend was not an expert at keeping patient records, and was using a bookkeeper who was aged and contemplating retirement.

Dr. Blanding's secretary also was something to be desired, so all these quirks were prying on Ken's mind. He hesitated bringing up the subject, since he'd been there such a short time, but if he was going to do his job in the best possible way, he needed a good, reliable secretary and filing clerk. Also, something would obviously have to be done with the bookkeeper.

When he first came to talk about the position, Dr. Blanding had told Ken that they would enlarge or rearrange the office to meet any of the needs Ken desired.

That morning was slow, so Ken thought it was a good time to approach the subject.

"Dr. John, you said if I needed added space, I was to tell you and we would rearrange the first floor for extra offices," Ken began.

"That's right, Ken," Dr. John nodded. "What've you got in mind?"

"First of all, I need a *good* secretary, one I can depend on at all times," Ken announced. "One that will keep accurate, confidential records, file them where both she and I can find them, and a nurse to help me prepare patients for the examining rooms. In that way, we would see twice as many patients in the office each day. We would also be freer to take on emergency calls for home and hospital if we have a competent staff here," Ken explained.

"It sounds fine to me," Dr. John nodded, "but where do you propose to find these indispensable people?"

"It won't be easy, I know," Ken admitted. "We will advertise, I suppose, then cull them out as they answer the ad. We may not keep the first one we hire, but we will make it clear there will be a thirty-day trial period. Using this method,.we will finally retain the girls who best qualify."

"Go ahead. Do whatever you need to enlarge the offices, and put ads in the local newspapers, and maybe out of town, too, if you like. Getting a good Registered Nurse will be the hardest."

"She doesn't have to be a Registered Nurse, Dr. John," Ken replied. "She can be a good technician and we can train her as to the qualifications we need of her. Her salary won't be as high as an R.N., and that way we can pay a higher wage and get a good conscientious secretary-receptionist. If we advertise for a medical secretary, she'll be trained in all the medical terms, and by using a technician, we can pay our secretary a higher salary. I assure you we'll get better service."

"It's a deal," Dr. John agreed. "You will have to take the responsibility, though. I'm getting weaker. The pain is beginning, and I'll need to take some treatments. They can be drastic at times, by draining the last drop of energy out of a fellow."

Ken had never asked Dr. John exactly what his problem was, since he thought if the doctor wanted Ken to know he'd tell him. He was, however, curious to know just where it was that Dr. Blanding's cancer was located. He suspected the intestinal area, but couldn't be sure.

"Another thing, Ken," Dr. John continued, and Ken snapped back to reality. "Old Joe Bain, my bookkeeper, wants to retire. He's been after me for years to get someone to do the books. What do you think of using a firm that does mainly doctors' accounts?"

"Fine," Ken nodded. "Do you know of one?"

"Yes, there are several here in the city, and I'll inquire around among some of my friends and get a recommendation from them."

"Great," Ken grinned. "Now I better get to the hospital and make rounds."

Ken left the house with more enthusiasm than he had been able to muster up for a long time. It didn't last long, however, for it was a short time later that he received the call from Sam Shaw and the news about Alex Ann's accident.

CHAPTER 5

When Ken came out of his reverie into the past, the shadows were lengthening across the lawn. He was surprised that no patients had called that afternoon, and no one had bothered him for several hours.

He immediately set to work on the problem at hand. The first step, he decided, was to find the best possible surgeon in the city and make arrangements for him to take Alex Ann's case. Dr. John would know; if not, he would surely know someone who did know a reliable man in the neurological field.

When Ken confronted Dr. Blanding with his dilemma, Dr. John replied, "Ken, in the first place, you're playing with fire. Alex is angry enough at you for running away from her. She would never consent to come to Pittsburgh."

"Her parents aren't going to tell her," Ken said in a tight voice. "They're only going to tell her they are moving her to another hospital with proper facilities."

"And you don't think she'll question them?" Dr. John demanded.

"Probably will," Ken admitted, "but Sam and Mervice think they can handle that situation."

"They'll never get away with it. As soon as she arrives, she'll know she's in a different climate. It won't take her long to discover where she's at."

"Nevertheless, she won't have to see me. I'll stay completely in the background," Ken vowed.

"You'll never convince her, unless she's so desperate and wants very badly to be active again. I doubt that, since you've already told me that she's lost all will to try."

"Dr. John, we have to try," Ken pleaded, feeling desperate. He had thought of all the good times he'd had with Alex Ann. Even though she was a selfish, thoughtless, domineering young woman, he wanted the best for her. "Do you know a neurosurgeon, one we can trust to do the very best for Alex?"

"Yes, I do," Dr. John nodded. "His specialty is spinal surgery, but he's not here right now. He went to Europe about two months ago and I'm not sure when he expects to return."

"Wouldn't you know it!" Ken exclaimed. "Just when we need him!"

"Now, calm down, Ken, and let's talk about it," Dr. John soothed.

"Who is he?" Ken demanded. "How can we find out when he'll be back? Would he fly back if we requested his services?" Ken was extremely agitated. What would happen if they couldn't locate him? Would they have to settle for second best? No way. Sam would never agree to that.

"Now, just slow down a bit, I said," Dr. John ordered. "His name is Dr. William Barkley, and his office is downtown near the West End Hospital. I'll call there and talk with one of his associates to see what we can work out."

Dr. John was used to such emergencies, and knew it took time to work out the many details before the patient could be seen.

Dr. Barkley's office contained three other surgeons who worked closely with him in all fields of neurosurgery. The receptionist connected Dr. John with the office of Dr. Peters. Dr. John asked the nurse who answered the telephone when Dr. Barkley would return.

"When he left, he planned to be gone six months," the nurse answered. "He is attending a series of seminars and the last one will be over in July. Could one of the other doctors help you? I'd be glad to connect you with Dr. Peters, who is Dr. Barkley's associate."

"Very well, thank you," said Dr. Blanding. "I'll speak with him."

"Hello, Dr. Blanding, this is Dr. Robert Peters," a male voice said. "What can I do to help you?"

Dr. Blanding explained the situation, even to the point of the possibility that Alex Ann might be a hostile patient, because of her association with Dr. Minard.

"Dr. Peters, do you think there's a chance that Dr. Barkley could fly back to the United States long enough to perform the surgery, then have you or one of his other colleagues take over so he could return to Europe to finish his task there?" Dr. Blanding pleaded.

"It's entirely possible, but before he would even consider such a drastic step, he would want to know a lot more about the case," Dr. Peters replied.

"What would you suggest?"

"Bring Miss Shaw here. We'll evaluate her case, in order to have something concrete to tell Dr. Barkley. It's possible that I or one of the other neurosurgeons could handle the case and Dr. Barkley wouldn't need to return."

"Thanks ever so much, Dr. Peters," Dr. Blanding answered. "I'll consult with the family and Dr. Minard. We'll be in touch."

"I'll do all I can to help, Dr. Blanding. You're quite a famous personality here in our city," Dr. Peters admitted. He didn't know that in a few months, or a year or two, Dr. Blanding would not be with them.

Dr. Blanding hung up the phone, then reported his conversation with Dr. Peters to Ken.

"They'll never settle for anything less than the best," Ken sighed. "Alex is their only child, and they'll use every dime to see that she gets top priority."

"Well, call them and tell them to bring Alex to Pittsburgh as quickly as possible. We'll explain the situation to Mr. and Mrs. Shaw and let Dr. Peters take it from there. But you must remain in the background," Dr. John cautioned, "and not antagonize Alex Ann or upset her any more than she is."

"You know I won't do that, Dr. John. I'll do all I can for both Alex and her parents."

The following Monday afternoon, at two fifty-nine, the plane landed at the Greater Pittsburgh Airport. Alex Ann was transferred to an ambulance and rushed to West End Hospital in downtown Pittsburgh.

Ken and Dr. Blanding met the plane, but Ken didn't allow Alex to catch sight of him. Mervice Shaw rode in the ambulance with Alex and the attendants. Sam came along in Ken's car with Dr. Blanding. Alex was taken to the neurosurgical wing, and the family was introduced to Dr. Rob Peters.

Dr. Peters explained that Dr. Barkley was out of the country and that with their permission he, Dr. Peters, would take her case, have tests run and after consultation with other doctors in the field they would give the parents a report. The main information they would seek was if surgery was necessary. If so, could Dr. Peters handle the case? If not, they would discuss calling Dr. Barkley.

Sam and Mervice agreed to his suggestion.

"May we see Alex Ann now?" Mervice asked.

"Certainly; visiting hours end at four-thirty p.m., and begin again at seven p.m. Have you made arrangements for living quarters while you're here?"

"Dr. Minard has taken care of that, and we'll stay as long as necessary even if I have to commute periodically," Sam Shaw stated firmly. "Alexandria is our only child and very important to us."

"Fine," Dr. Peters nodded. "I'll talk to you again tomorrow."

"Thank you, Dr. Peters, and you, Dr. Blanding, for all you've done for us."

"Don't give me the credit," Dr. John laughed. "This Dr. Minard is a slave driver. He's quite a boy."

Alex Ann was in a very cheery hospital room on the fifth floor. When her parents walked in, she exclaimed, "Traitors! Why did you bring me here? Why didn't I go to Gainesville? You brought me here because of Ken, and I don't want anything to do with him."

"It's true that Ken made the arrangements, but it was Dr. Blanding who assured us that the best neurosurgeons we could have were here. Tomorrow morning, one of them, Dr. Rob Peters, will be in to talk with you. As far as Ken is concerned, he has promised not to come near you if that is really your wish," her mother explained in a soothing tone. "He's a busy man, Alex, and has taken on a big responsibility, but you were his main concern when he heard you were in an accident."

Alex softened a little, then said, "Oh, Daddy, do you think they can help me here? Is there a chance I'll walk again?"

"We'll see, Alexandria, darling," he calmed her. "We won't know until Dr. Peters has examined you and consulted with his colleagues. Now, Mother and I are going to our tourist home, unpack and freshen up. We'll be back for evening visiting hours."

"Our quarters are just a block from the hospital," Mervice commented, "and it will be convenient for both Dad and me to drop in to see you. We can also eat breakfast there. It will be quite comfortable, not at all like living in a motel."

She hugged Alex, and the two adults left. Ken was waiting to drive them to the big, white two-story house, where they would stay for the duration of Alex Ann's illness. The couple was pleased with the accommodations, and with the lovely landlady who welcomed them in the true Pennsylvania manner.

Alexandria Ann didn't sleep very well her first night in the hospital. The plane trip had been nerve-wracking, and the thought of her parents deceiving her by bringing her here where Ken was, made her so angry she couldn't sleep.

Ken had his work cut out for him, interviewing nurses and receptionist-secretaries and remodeling the new offices. Besides, he would want to check on Alex's progress each day, but he would do it through her parents.

Unlike Alex, Ken slept soundly that night. Fortunately, the phone didn't ring once.

The ads that Dr. Minard placed in the local newspapers were short, but precise:

> One medical technician to work in doctor's office. Not necessary to be R.N. Will train.
>
> One medical secretary-receptionist. Must have some experience in medical terminology, pleasant

personality, and be able to meet people, make appointments and be emotionally stable.

A telephone number was also added. He had no idea how many applicants he would receive, if any, but time would tell.

Carpenters were already at work on the offices. It was only a matter of a partition here, some paneling there, new draperies to brighten up the windows, new carpeting, desks and various office equipment. In the other offices, Ken needed plumbing and cabinets along with examining tables, shelves for supplies, scales for weighing and a roll stool and chairs for the waiting patients.

He decided that the records would be kept in full tab manila folders, one for each patient. They would be filed alphabetically, standing on end with the tab to the outside, on open shelves built against the wall on one side of the secretary's office. Displayed in this manner, the folder could be detected in an instant and removed until the patients were examined, then filed in place as quickly at the end of office hours, or once a day at closing time, whichever the secretary preferred. Previously, Dr. Blanding had used a card filing system, which proved most inefficient.

The ad appeared in the morning papers, and that afternoon Ken interviewed four girls—two technicians and two secretaries. Neither of the technicians was suitable for the position. One felt she wasn't up to the grueling hours, and the other was not highly trained and would have needed someone to work with her for a while. Ken couldn't afford that. He eliminated both girls.

The secretary-receptionists were just about as bad. One was a medical secretary and very good in her field, but she didn't want to combine the two positions. She felt a doctor's office should have a regular receptionist as well as a medical secretary.

It might come to that later on, but for the time being, one girl would need to do both jobs.

Ken explained that financially it wasn't feasible, and she declined the position.

The next girl was the daughter of a realtor in Pittsburgh. Her name was Caroline Wells.

"What experience do you have in the medical field?" Ken asked. "Can you file records, answer the telephone and meet people?"

"I have had no experience at all," she replied quite calmly.

"Then why did you answer my ad?" Ken asked, perplexed. "You're a very beautiful young lady, but I need more than that for this job. You should be doing something like modeling for *Vogue* magazine."

"Thank you very much for the compliment," the girl replied, "but I have no interest in modeling. I would like to work in your office."

"You have no experience, in either medical or regular clerical work, yet you answered the ad. Why is that?" he asked. "Why would you think I would even consider you?"

"I didn't suppose you would," she answered truthfully, "but you see, I'm bright, I love people and can talk to them quite easily. I can type, file and answer the phone. It's true I'm not familiar with medical terms, but I could learn. I'd get a dictionary, and look up every word if I had to." Caroline was sure Dr. Minard was angry with her, and she began to wonder why she'd even come. She wanted to grab her purse and flee before he said another word.

"That still doesn't answer my question," Ken persisted.

"All right, I'll level with you," she sighed. "My father is Roy Wells, one of the wealthiest realtors in Allegheny County. I have always had everything I needed or wanted. Clothes, cars, boyfriends—you name it, I have it—except for one thing."

"What is that?" Ken questioned, curious.

"A purpose in life," she announced. "Something I can do for myself. A job that I get paid for because I'm doing something worthwhile. Association with humanity, not just all those old social busybody friends of mothers. All my girl friends run around in circles. They just put in their time. They accomplish nothing at all constructive. I'm tired of that. I'd like to change my way of life." She got up to leave. "I guess I'm just not qualified for your office, and maybe not for any other, either. Maybe there's nothing I can do."

"Caroline Wells, starting next Monday morning—if the carpenters get finished as they've promised—you will be my new secretary-receptionist," Ken announced suddenly.

"Honest!" the girl exclaimed, staring at the man in disbelief. "You're not fooling? You'd really take a chance on me?"

"I can't think of one reason why I should," he admitted. "Maybe I'm nuts, but, yes, I'm willing to take a chance on you. It may be rough for both of us, but I'm hiring a technician also, if I can find one, and maybe the three of us can manage to keep the doors open."

"Oh, thank you, Dr. Minard," the girl bubbled. "I just can't believe it. I'll work my fingers to the bones, and I'll try not to make any more mistakes than I can help."

"Everyone makes mistakes, Miss Wells, even doctors. Would it be all right if I called you Caroline? I don't like this Miss, Mrs. or Mr. business."

"Yes, sir, Doctor, you can call me whatever you like. I'll be here Monday morning at eight-thirty sharp," she promised. "Good-bye, Doctor, and thank you...oh, thank you so much!"

What is happening to me? Ken wondered after the girl had left his office. *I've been out of touch for four years, just returned the past two months and now, against my better judgment, I've hired a secretary with no experience. She sure is beautiful, though. Careful, there, boy, that's strong medicine for such a weak man!* he warned himself.

The next young woman who applied for the technician's job was just what Ken needed. She was quick thinking and responded just as rapidly. Besides having a lovely personality, she needed the job. For that reason, Ken felt she would be conscientious.

The following Monday morning, Caroline Wells and Mary Ann McCartney came to work for Dr. Ken Minard and Dr. John Blanding.

Dr. John wasn't used to all the hustle and bustle of secretaries and technicians. Deep down he resented being run over by progress. He then remembered his fate in life and knew that if Ken was to take over his practice, he, Dr. John, would have to "come to the party." He would have to adjust as best he could. Maybe he could spend most of his time at the hospital or doing house calls, and let the young folks do the hard work.

Too, he wanted to keep his eye on Alex Ann Shaw. It was only through him that Ken could obtain the professional opinions on Alex. Sam and Mervice would keep him up to date, but not in the same way as Dr. Blanding.

The first day with his new office staff was bedlam for Ken. The girls did their best to keep things under control. Everything moved ever so slowly. There was a multitude of patients and with each passing hour they got further behind. It was something that couldn't be helped. The day wore on, with each patient grumbling more than the last, until Dr. Ken took time to explain the situation and then most of the patients apologized and commended Ken for his patience.

Mary Ann McCartney was an excellent nurse-technician. She seemed to contemplate Dr. Minard's every move. She learned his methods quickly, and by the end of the first week she was a pro.

Caroline wasn't doing quite so well. There was a flood of patients and she needed to work out a system so she could get everything done as quickly as possible. It was a real struggle for her, and by the end of the first week she thought, *How did I get into this mess? Whatever made me think I could handle this job?*

When the last patient left on Friday afternoon, she collapsed in her office chair, hysterically tired.

"What's up, Caroline?" Dr. Ken asked. "You tired?"

"I give up," Caroline moaned faintly. "I just can't do it. I'm completely exhausted."

"Yes, you *can* do it," he insisted. "This is only the first week. It will take you at least three months to get completely organized. Don't give up so easily. Next week Mary Ann and I will help you a little more. We'll see if we can work out a better plan. Okay?"

"I guess so," she nodded, "if you still want me to plug along."

"Could I make a suggestion?" Mary Ann asked, coming into the room.

"Any suggestions will be appreciated at this time," Dr. Ken stated. "What's your idea?"

"Well, I can type, and I'm familiar with the medical terms used. To relieve Caroline a little at first, until she gets the files and such organized, I could do some of the charts for her. If you," she looked at Dr. Minard, "could purchase a small tape recorder, and after each examination and diagnosis, before you see the next patient, dictate the information onto the tape. Then, while you're making hospital rounds, I could type up the records, or at least the greatest portion of them, and help Caroline file them when we have a few free minutes. I might be able to catch the phone for her sometimes, too, if she'd like. In this way, between the two of us, we'd keep things up-to-date each day."

"How about it, Caroline?" Ken asked, looking to her for approval.

"Great," she replied, much relieved. "I'm so busy making up new files, arranging appointments and ten hundred other things that I'd welcome any help I could get."

"Okay, girls, it's all yours," Ken announced. "Two heads are always better than one, and I'll abide by whatever arrangements you can work out."

"Since we have no patients on Saturday morning, would it be all right if I came in then and worked until noon?" Caroline asked. "I could accomplish a great deal with no one around."

"Suit yourself," Ken nodded. "It's a great idea, and I could compensate by raising your salary a few cents," he said, laughingly.

"That won't be necessary, Doctor. When I think I deserve a raise, I'll ask for it," Caroline replied. "Until then, give me the freedom of working overtime if I choose."

"You are really remarkable, Caroline," Ken stated. "Of course, I'll go along with whatever you decide." *How did I ever find such a jewel among so many stray stones?* Ken wondered to himself.

The office routine of Minard and Blanding progressed until it ran so smoothly that nobody would have guessed the two girls were so inexperienced when they first began working in the office.

CHAPTER 6

Alex Ann had been in the hospital for six weeks. The neurosurgeons had disputed the diagnosis of the doctors at the Tampa hospital. Her injury was not as severe as the Shaws had been led to believe; therefore, surgery was not indicated.

Dr. Rob Peters was sure from all the tests taken that Alex Ann would be able to walk again if she could have the right kind of therapy, and if she was willing to work hard.

Alex was a very hostile patient at first, but began to mellow a little. She even agreed to see Ken.

"Do you have faith in Dr. Peters?" she asked Ken. "He says surgery isn't necessary, and that with the right therapy I should be able to walk, at least with a walker."

"Yes, Alex, I have complete faith in Dr. Peters," Ken nodded. "He knows what he's doing. If you follow his instructions, you'll probably get much better."

"But I want to walk, like I used to, and drive a car, and water ski, and do all the things I did before," Alex moaned.

Ken was tempted to remind her that she should have thought of that before she sped down the road at a hundred miles an hour. Instead, he said, "Let's take one thing at a time, and pray your wishes will come true." Ken wasn't very reassuring, for at the time there was no way anyone could be sure of the outcome of Alex's condition.

"He said he was assigning me to a therapist by the name of Dr. Bill Brant," Alex stated. "Do you know him?"

"Yes, I know Dr. Brant," Ken replied. "He's the head therapist in the neurological wing. You'll like him. He's thorough and may be hard on you, but he has a sense of humor. Most of the nurses refer to him as a 'living doll.' He's a handsome man, and very capable in his field."

Bill Brant was a doctor because his father wanted him to be one. He'd had a tough struggle through medical school. His career was interrupted by the draft, and when he worked in the Navy hospitals he became interested in rehabilitation of the men with near permanent injuries. He was given a special assignment in the field, and when his time was up he went back to his home town to try to find a position in physiotherapy. West End Hospital interviewed and accepted him almost immediately.

Dr. Brant was five feet ten inches tall, a blond with freckles. He was a little on the chunky side and, as Ken had related to Alex, had a great sense of humor. Things came slowly to him, but when he mastered them, he was the best.

His greatest fear was that he would get a patient for whom he could do nothing. If he couldn't see progress, he was stymied, even though he'd been indoctrinated from the beginning of his career that it could happen. He had a great success rate, though, and wanted to keep it that way. Dr. Minard was aware of all this, and could assure Alex she had nothing to worry about.

"They want to start tomorrow," she divulged. "I'm scared...I guess I'm just chicken," she admitted. "I'm afraid the pain will be excruciating."

"Grit your teeth, take one step at a time, and above all, have the determination to fight," Ken instructed.

"Thanks, Ken. I'm sorry I've been so rotten to you," she said shyly. "You really are a wonderful person. How are things going in your practice?" she asked.

"Dr. Blanding is getting weaker. I'm trying to carry as much of the load as I can," Ken replied. "I just hired a secretary and a technician to help out in the office, so Dr. John will have less physical work to do. This will leave him free for consultation. I still have a great deal to learn, and it's a twenty-four-hour job. So you'll have to forgive me, Alex Ann, if I don't get to visit you as often as I'd like. I'll try to run by once in a while, and I'll keep in touch through your parents," he promised. "Bye, for now, Alex, and remember...determination."

"I'll remember," Alex nodded, then said, quite seriously, "Say a prayer for me, please."

Ken was a little more than surprised that Alex would mention prayer. He'd never heard her express a belief in any faith. He wondered if she knew how to pray or if she even knew the meaning of the word.

"That I can do," he nodded. "I've said many prayers for you. Perhaps you'll do the same for me. Pray that I'll have the ability and strength to stand up under my enormous task. I'll see you later."

It was easy for Ken to pray, for he'd turned to God daily in his life, as well as the loss of his parents, the struggle to get through school and the war he'd gone through. Prayer was nothing new to Ken. He wondered how new it might be to Alex Ann.

After Ken left, Alex thought, *How could I have ever doubted him? Why was I mean and hateful? He's doing a tremendous job, and I hope that someday he will find a girl he truly loves, marry her and live happily ever after.*

Alex Ann realized she wasn't meant to be that girl, and for a time she was sad for herself as well as Ken. She then breathed a prayer for herself, for Ken, and for the Dr. Brant who was going to help her walk again.

It was a tremendous challenge for Dr. Brant to be assigned to Alexandria Ann Shaw's case. If he could help her to walk again, he would realize his dream.

The treatments began and continued through the spring. With spring, came the rain, slush, mud and high rivers that were typical of Pittsburgh and all of western Pennsylvania that time of year. May was usually a beautiful month, and that year was no exception.

Ken Minard continued to work hard, and Dr. John took some treatments to see if the cancer could be arrested, even if for a short time. Most of the time, he was too sick to work, as the treatments were so severe that they left him completely exhausted.

Dr. Ken, Caroline and Mary Ann were seeing about thirty-five patients a day. The staff was completely exhausted when evening came, so there was little time for socializing for any of them.

Mary Ann seemed to have an endless amount of energy, and always succeeded in finishing her daily tasks. Caroline got behind once in a while, and had to work on Saturdays to catch up. Ken looked in on her on those mornings, and gave her all the encouragement he could. He never failed to notice how strikingly beautiful she was, yet she was so conscientious. She loved the job and told him so, many times.

One Saturday morning, a young mother with a two-year-old boy rushed into the office. Luckily, Ken was there, and so was Caroline.

The child had a bad laceration on his left leg. Ken treated it, then suggested that the mother take him to the emergency room at the hospital, where a surgeon would suture the wound.

After they'd gone, Caroline asked Ken, "Would you like me to help you clean the office? Then you'll be free to go if an emergency call comes in."

"Okay, fine," Dr. Ken agreed. "That's very thoughtful of you."

The two worked diligently for the next hour or so, and when everything was in order and Caroline was about to leave, Ken remarked, "I hope you know how much I appreciate your help this morning and every day. I'd like to compensate in some way."

"That isn't necessary, Doctor," Caroline shook her head. "I do it because...." She couldn't finish. She couldn't tell Dr. Minard that she was falling in love with him. She was only a secretary, and not a very good one at that, and office romances often turned out to be tragedies.

"Why, Caroline?" Ken persisted. "Why do you work overtime and do all the things that aren't required of you?"

"I can't tell you, Doctor," Caroline stated. "I just can't, that's all."

At that moment, Ken put his arms around Caroline, and she melted against him, helpless to resist his advances.

"Is it because you feel the same way about me as I do about you?" he asked, softly. "I love you, Caroline, and I had to tell you...I couldn't let it go any longer. Do you care for me?"

"Yes, I've loved you, I think, since the beginning," Caroline admitted. Ken kissed her, but she pulled away. "Now I will have to leave my job. We won't be able to work together anymore," she announced.

"Why not, for heaven's sake?" Ken demanded, puzzled. "What's being in love got to do with your job?"

"People will suspect, Mary Ann will notice and Dr. John will know," Caroline said sadly.

"Don't kid yourself," Ken smiled. "Mary Ann has already suspected that we were attracted to each other. Dr. John will be elated. He's always preaching that I should find a girl, get married and have a decent home life."

"Oh, Ken," Caroline murmured, using his Christian name for the first time. "I love you so, and I'm so happy. I can't wait to tell everyone."

"Everyone?" Ken questioned. "Who's everyone?"

"My parents, my friends...everyone," she bubbled.

"Wait a minute. Don't you think I should meet your parents first and let them get to know me a little before you spring this revelation on them?" he asked, amused.

"I guess you're right," she admitted. "It's just that I'm so excited!" she exclaimed. She threw her arms around Ken and kissed him ravenously. "I'll ask mother to invite you to dinner. Will you come?"

"Yes, of course, if I'm not called out on an emergency, or have to sit with a sick cat, or any of the many other things I do," he grinned.

"Oh, you're silly," Caroline laughed. "You never sit with sick cats." Then she sobered. "What about your parents? How will we tell them?"

"My parents are dead, Caroline," Ken said quietly. "Dr. John is really the only family I have, besides the Shaws."

"What about Alex Ann? She's always liked you."

"We are only good friends, and I'm sure she'll be happy for me," Ken answered. "So, now, young lady..." he kissed her hard on the mouth, "let's close up this office and get some lunch. Or...will you have lunch with me, Miss Wells?" he asked.

"I'd be delighted, Dr. Minard, just delighted." She rushed off to clear her desk and lock up.

The general practitioner in Pennsylvania, especially in small towns, is not accustomed to taking days and evenings off. In Florida, however, the doctors never have evening hours and, as a general rule, they see patients only four or four-and-a-half days each week.

It was quite an adjustment for Ken. so when Caroline asked him to the Wells' mansion on Squirrel Hill for dinner and to meet her parents, he had to secure a standby.

Dr. Blanding was taking cobalt treatments and was not up to par for a few days after each treatment, so Ken couldn't depend on him to cover the patients.

He had met a lot of doctors in the months since he's come to Pittsburgh, so he contacted one of them and the doctor offered to stand by if Ken agreed to return the favor at a later date.

Ken had never been so nervous in his life, not even when he gave speeches during the time he was in the Florida Senate.

Should I wear evening clothes? he wondered. *Do they dress for dinner, or can I just wear an executive's suit and tie as is my custom?* He'd forgotten to ask Caroline, and it was now too late to contact her. He would have to improvise.

He chose a matched polyester jacket and slacks of a smooth weave, and a striped shirt with a plain tie.

If they're in evening clothes, I'll die, he thought. *Surely Mr. Wells won't dress for dinner after working in an office all day.*

Dinner was at eight, a little later than Ken was used to eating his evening meal. A cup of coffee with sugar would give him a burst of energy and hold him until dinner was served. He dashed into the kitchen and asked Quinter to pour him a cup of coffee. He put two teaspoonsful of sugar in it and consumed it so quickly that Quinter remarked, "Coffee was designed to drink, not inhale."

"Thank you, Quinter, but I'm in a terrible hurry," Ken explained.

"The only thing that would be so important to a doctor, besides a sick patient, is a beautiful girl," Quinter observed.

"You're so smart, ol' man, so smart," Ken nodded. Then he was off to his bedroom to dress.

As he drove through the heavy evening traffic, Ken wondered what the Wells home would be like. Would they like him, would he like them? Were they as rich as everyone supposed? Just then he came upon a big brick-cased, two-story house set on a large corner lot on Squirrel Hill.

His first thought was, *They're as rich as everyone says.*

The home was magnificent, and each house, on each block, in every direction, was of the same elegant type of architecture. He turned into the circular drive, which came up to an enormous front porch with a heavy carved wooden door. Other cars were parked in the drive, but he assumed it would be all right to leave his there.

When he rang the doorbell, he expected a butler to answer, but he was surprised to see Caroline open the door.

She took him by the hand, and said, "I asked Jason to let me answer the door. I knew it was you. You look absolutely marvelous. I hope you had no difficulty finding our place." Caroline looked up to him with a questioning look.

"No, finding you was no problem, but the environment is breathtaking. We have some beautiful homes in Tampa, but none to compare with this. And you...you look stunning," he said.

Caroline spent hours studying all her wardrobe, talking out loud to herself about what she was going to wear. She finally chose a blue polyester A-line with long flowing sheer sleeves and an overskirt of the same sheer nylon, silver slippers, and a waist-long silver chain necklace with matching bracelet. Her long, blonde hair was piled high on her head and she had a single silver clip at the nape of her neck.

Ken seemed glued to the spot. Caroline looked ravishing. He couldn't believe she was his secretary.

"Well, don't just stand there," she chided happily. "Come into the sitting room and meet my parents before Jason calls us for dinner." She swirled around excitedly.

"I just want to stand here and look at you. You're so lovely and different, not at all like my efficient secretary," he attempted to explain.

"I dressed like this on purpose," Caroline admitted. "I wanted you to be surprised."

"Mission accomplished," Ken murmured as they walked toward the sitting room.

They went from the foyer into an entrance room with a circular staircase and a balcony above. From either side of the room one could enter the stairway, cross the balcony, and come down to the other side. Ken assumed the bedrooms all opened off of the balcony.

"Mother, Father, this is Dr. Ken Minard," Caroline introduced them. "Ken, these are my parents, Christine and Roy Wells."

Mrs. Wells curtsied and her husband extended his hand to Ken, shook it heartily and then everyone sat down.

Ken wanted desperately to look around the room and drink in all the marvelous furnishings, but he felt it would be too obvious, so he tried to keep his attention on the person speaking.

"Caroline has spoken of you often," Mrs. Wells stated.

"Often!" Roy Wells blasted. "That's all she ever talks about...you and that job of hers. We tried to discourage her from working, as she is very well provided for."

"She should be socializing and having a good time while she's still young, but all our suggestions fell on deaf ears," her mother inserted.

"I'm glad, for my sake, that that happened," Ken admitted. "Caroline is a very efficient secretary, and our patients all like her poise and humble approach to them," he assured Mrs. Wells.

"Nevertheless, I still think she's wasting her time. If she wanted to work, she could have helped a few days a month in my office," Roy Wells said boisterously.

"I don't like the real estate business, Daddy. Besides, I would have seen too much of you and that wouldn't have worked. I needed time to myself to prove I could do something on my own besides being a social butterfly," Caroline explained.

As the conversation was beginning to make Ken uneasy, Jason announced that dinner was served.

Christine Wells took Ken's arm and led him to the huge dining room, above which hung the most beautiful and elegant chandelier Ken had ever seen. Since there were only four of them, they sat opposite each other at the table. Roy Wells was at the head of the table, Christine Wells at the opposite end, and Ken and Caroline on either side.

Ken's worries about his dress were needless, as he discovered that Roy Wells was wearing a very expensive business suit, and Christine a plain, long, pale green formal.

Mrs. Wells, like Caroline, was a beautiful woman, and had kept her petite figure splendidly for her age.

During the course of the dinner, Ken came to the conclusion that Roy Wells was a perfect specimen for a coronary. He was overweight, smoked smelly cigars and gorged himself with food.

Dinner went well, and Ken and Caroline left afterwards to go to a club for the balance of the evening to dance and be alone for a while. It seemed odd to be in a setting such as this, when just that morning they were in white uniforms. Ken thought it was pleasant to be alone with such a lovely creature, dressed perfectly for the occasion.

Her eyes were the loveliest thing about her—large, round and as blue as the Florida sky. They were captivating and devilish, and Ken had trouble keeping his mind where it belonged.

As they danced, Caroline whispered, "I hope they liked you. I think mother was quite taken with you. She likes all handsome men, and tries to make a good impression on them."

"Your father is quite a card," Ken admitted. "He says what he thinks, and I like that in a man. You know exactly where you stand. Do you suppose I made a good impression on him?"

"Well...if you didn't I'll find out soon enough," Caroline replied slowly. "As soon as I get home, he'll explode if he thinks I shouldn't see you anymore."

"Don't say that," Ken groaned. "I won't sleep a wink and we have a big day tomorrow. You will tell me the truth about how they do feel, won't you?" he asked.

"Yes, of course, I will; but, oh, darling, they just have to love you as much as I do. I couldn't stand it if they didn't."

The evening came to a close. Ken took Caroline home, and as he went to bed, he thought out loud, "I must win this family over. Dr. John has always said, 'Be yourself,' and that's what I tried to do."

Ken tossed and turned a while, then finally fell asleep. It seemed as if the alarm rang too soon and another day was about to begin in the offices of Doctors Blanding and Minard.

CHAPTER 7

The months wore on, and Dr. John continued to lose ground. Alex Ann wasn't much better. Ken Minard was worn out from the rigorous schedule that general practitioners have to follow.

Sam and Mervice Shaw were faithful in their visits and concern for Alex. Sam commuted between Pittsburgh and Tampa when necessary, but it was already September, and cold weather would soon be coming to Pennsylvania again. September and October were their favorite months in the north and although it wasn't easy, they found ways to entertain themselves between visits to the hospital.

Mervice was a compulsive knitter, and had made three garments since arriving in Pittsburgh. Then she spent hours shopping. Pittsburgh had stores comparable to Miami, and it was fun to browse through them. She made friends with other women on the block during the summer months, and they attended plays and went to the motion pictures when Sam was away. Mervice had spent only two full weeks at home in Tampa since Alex's's accident.

Time and expense were beginning to wear on them, but they were, like many parents, victims of circumstance. They had a crippled child, and they stood by while the experts worked, endlessly, to help her walk again.

Alex Ann felt she wasn't making any progress in therapy. She had worked so hard and Dr. Bill kept encouraging her to "try again," "try harder," "work longer." It wasn't any use. Alex Ann was depressed. Was it possible that she no longer wanted to get well?

When the nurse came to get her in the wheelchair that always transported her to the therapy floor, Alex said, "I'm not going today. It's no use. I'm no better than before."

"Oh, yes, you are, Miss Shaw," the nurse replied firmly. "Now you remember that some time ago you couldn't even sit up. Dr. Brant says you are his last patient today and he will be able to spend a little more time with you."

"You mean I'll be the only patient there this afternoon?" Alex Ann asked, perking up.

"Yes, Dr. Brant left you until last today."

Maybe I can be alone with Dr. Bill today, Alex Ann thought, as her heart jumped. *Maybe I'll have a chance to find out how he really feels about me. Wouldn't it be wonderful if he really cared for me? How could he, though? I'm a cripple, and nobody wants a cripple.*

"Okay, nurse," she said out loud, "let's go. But I think it's hopeless."

Dr. Bill Brant glanced at his schedule and discovered he had only one more patient that day—Alex Ann Shaw.

Alex must try harder, he thought. *She has to get well and walk again.*

When Alex was put in his care, Bill Brant found a tremendous challenge, but he hadn't counted on falling in love with her. It crept up on him like a fog and enveloped him to the suffocating point. It was entirely possible that Bill Brant didn't realize, as yet, what was happening to him.

Nurse Bell entered with Alex Ann, just as Dr. Brant's last patient was leaving. The other therapists had also gone

"Would you like me to stay and help, Dr. Brant?" the nurse offered. "I'll be glad to stand by if you need me."

"No, thank you, Miss Bell. I can handle Miss Shaw by myself. She's making real progress, and maybe one of these days we'll be losing her. I'll ring when I'm ready for you to take her back."

"It'll be wonderful if she can leave shortly, even though we'll miss her," Nurse Bell remarked, then left Alex Ann at the mercy of Dr. Bill Brant.

"Well, Alex, we're going to try something new today," Dr. Bill announced, as he wheeled her chair to the end of the ramp affair with two railings, one on each side. "We're going to walk this ramp today."

"I could never do that!" she protested. "I couldn't take two consecutive steps."

"How do you know that?" he demanded. "You haven't even tried yet." He stepped to the wheelchair. "Now, I will stand you up and you take a firm grip on the railings. I'll walk backwards ahead of you. If, at any time, you get tired or you feel you're going to fall, I'll catch you. Now, don't be afraid. Will you try?"

"I'll try anything once," Alex said, reluctantly.

"Okay, here goes. Hold on with both hands and come towards me," Dr. Bill instructed. He stood Alex up, saw that she got both hands firmly on the bars, then said, "Now, take a step. Use your arms to help. Good...now, another one."

"My legs are so weak," she complained. "They feel like they're not there."

"I know, that's why we have to exercise them," Bill commented. "Come on, take another step."

"I can't, Doctor, I just can't," Alex pleaded.

"Yes, you can, come on...try, try, Alex. Try for me," Bill coaxed. Dr. Brant was calling her by her first name and a warm feeling penetrated her entire being.

At that point, Alex would have done anything for the man standing before her. She was so in love with him, but she was in a position where she could not let him know. If only he would make some gesture, she would have some reason to try...some reason to want to live. Was it possible that Dr. Brant cared for her even a little?

Alex took one step, then another, but when she tried to force her legs to take the third step, the weakness engulfed her and she started to lunge forward.

Bill saw her beginning to fall and he stepped up and caught her in his arms. He held her lightly for a second or two so that her feet barely touched the floor, then he whispered, "Are you okay?"

"Yes...I'm all right," she stammered. Alex was shaking all over, but her weakness was the result of Bill's closeness as much as the lifeless legs she was trying to stand on.

In that instant, Bill folded her into his arms. Her arms went around his neck, and for a minute they were too ecstatic to speak.

"I knew you could do it!" Bill finally spoke. "I knew you could walk! Oh, Alex, I love you, I love you so much I ache! I've loved you from that very first day. You have so much spirit, and I want so badly for you to walk."

"I was afraid you'd never say those words," Alex sighed. "I love you, too, and wanted you to hold me every day I came to therapy. I want you to hold me always."

"I promise I will," he whispered. "I'll never let you go." Then his lips were on hers, and she was almost fainting from the rapture of the closeness. Finally, Bill gently lowered Alex until she was resting on her feet.

"Now, I think we better get you back to the wheelchair and take you back to bed where you can rest. Do you realize you took three steps today, Alex?" he asked.

"All I know is that I have a reason to live again," she replied. "I don't want to go back to my room until you tell me when I can see you again."

"Anytime you want," Bill replied. "Just send word to me, and I'll be there," he vowed.

After the nurse wheeled out Alex, Bill thought, *She didn't really take three steps. She shuffled her legs along while she used the bars as crutches. Nevertheless, she made progress. She tried, and that's the first and most important step. She loves me, too. I can't believe it! She loves me as much as I do her!*

Then he prayed, "Oh, God, if you can hear me amidst all these machines and equipment, give me the knowledge to help Alex walk. Transmit your power to me and to Alex and help us not to give up until we have won."

Alex had been cautioned repeatedly by the medical staff not to attempt to get out of bed unassisted. However, she wasn't one of those individuals who took orders from others. She was used to being her own boss, and was so spoiled by her parents that she paid little attention to the staff's advice.

I'm sick of lying in this bed day after day, with nothing to do, she complained to herself. *If I'm going to walk, I'll have to get out of here and make some effort on my own. I'm sick of these doctors saying, "It will take time." How much time?* she wondered. After the day before on the ramp, she believed that maybe she could do it herself.

After her bath and bed change that morning, she had a revelation.

"Nurse, could you let down the sides of my bed this morning?" she asked sweetly. "I feel as if I'm in jail. I'll be very careful, I promise," she wheedled.

"It's against hospital rules in your case," the nurse replied sternly, but not unkindly. "I can't make an exception, even for you."

"All right, then, will you please close the door when you leave?" Alex Ann asked. "I'm going to take a little nap and don't want to be disturbed."

"Certainly," the nurse nodded. "If you need anything, just ring, and please don't try to get up by yourself," she warned.

Alex waited until she was sure there was no one around. Then she managed to lower the bed rail on the side of her bed. She shifted her body around so she could get her legs over the edge of the bed. If she could slide down to the floor—the bed was in the high position—the bed could be her resting post.

To Alex's sorrow, she had not considered the fact that her legs would not support her body, and beds have nothing much to hold onto except at the foot and the head. It meant she would be grasping the foot of the bed with just one hand.

When she eased herself off the bed, the pain, as usual, was unbearable. She began to slide faster than anticipated and because she had nothing to hold onto with her left hand, she fell crashing to the floor.

She hadn't thought about using the automatic device on the side of the bed that lowered the bed to a sitting position where she could have reached the floor unaided.

Screaming, "Nurse, nurse! Help me, help me!" she struggled to get her legs out from under herself, but she couldn't move.

The door was closed so the nursing staff could not hear her. Alex had chosen a private room because she didn't want anyone "spying" on her. She could have used a roommate at that moment.

"Please, help me!" she called frantically. "I can't get up! I can't stand the pain!"

Dr. Minard had been making rounds that morning and they took longer than usual. He should have been on his way back to the office, but he knew if he didn't stop to see Alex he would feel guilty all day.

It seemed as if hours passed, but it was only seconds when Ken came to the door of Room 307. He heard a moan and rushed through the door to find Alex sprawled on the floor, helpless as a baby.

"Help me, Ken," she groaned. "Oh, help me!"

"Alex, how did you manage to fall out of bed?" he demanded. "I thought they kept the sides up." Ken felt he shouldn't move Alex until the doctor in charge could be called.

He pressed the buzzer for the nurses' station and said, "This is Dr. Minard. Will you get Dr. Peters to Room 307 quickly? If he's not available, get Dr. Brant."

"Yes, right away, doctor," and the buzzer light went out.

Dr. Brant was there in seconds, and Dr. Minard helped him lift Alex into bed.

"Why were the sides left down on your bed, Alex?" Dr. Brant demanded. "I left specific orders that these rails were to be kept up at all times just so an incident like this didn't occur."

"Please, Bill, I asked the nurse to let the sides down," Alex Ann fibbed. "I felt like I was in jail."

"That's better than falling out of bed," he grumbled.

"Dr. Peters is going to be very disappointed with you, Alex. I can't do anything more for you until he is contacted and I receive further word from him," Dr. Brant announced.

"Alex, did you fall out of bed, or were you playing one of your well-known tricks behind the doctor's back?" Ken asked suddenly. "It's important. Please tell Dr. Brant the truth." He knew Alex well, and was aware that there was nothing she wouldn't try if she thought it necessary.

"He's right, Bill," Alex admitted after a short silence. "I tried to get out of bed by myself. I thought if I could try then maybe I could learn to walk," she cried.

"Well, the damage is done now," Dr. Brant snapped. "At this point, I'm quite disgusted with you. Now, we'll have to begin all over. If you were going to try such a dumb thing, why didn't you at least let your bed down as far as it would go and you wouldn't have fallen so far?" he questioned.

"I never thought of it," Alex mumbled through her tears. "'The best laid plans' always go haywire when one is trying to deceive someone. What now? Will it mean I may have undone all we've tried to accomplish?" A stricken look crossed her face.

"I don't know," Dr. Brant said, shaking his head. "That's for Dr. Peters to say, but for now I'm going to order you a sedative, see that the sides are up on your bed and from now on, young lady, I guess I'll have to station the Secret Service next to your bed!"

Oh, no, darling, Alex wanted to cry, *that won't be necessary. I'll be on my best behavior,* but she didn't want Ken to know about her feelings for Bill at that time.

"That's not necessary, Bill," she said out loud. "I'll do as you say. I've learned my lesson. Please forgive me." Her eyes pleaded with him.

Ken Minard left Room 307 wondering, *Has she really learned her lesson? Will Alex ever be able to conform or will her selfishness always rule her better judgment?*

Apparently Ken wasn't aware of the familiarity between Alex and Bill Brant, or if he was, he merely shrugged it off as another of Alex's personality traits.

The days went on, and Alex became stronger, but it would be a while before she could leave the hospital. She felt she should have more exercise, but Bill had other patients, and he couldn't see Alex on his time off.

She needs more therapy, Bill thought. *She needs different kinds, like leg exercises, walking with the aid of a walker and having someone with her. If we were married, I could spend more time with her. Then she would progress faster.*

When Alex came for therapy the next day, Bill seemed ecstatic.

"My, you are cheerful today, Dr. Bill Brant," Alex smiled. "What's so exciting?"

"Let's get married!" he announced.

"Married!" she cried. "I can't even walk and you want to get married!"

"Yes, I want to get married right away," he nodded firmly. "You see, if we were together all the time, I could give you a lot more exercises and therapy than you are getting here. You could leave the hospital, and while I'm on duty, your mother could be with you. After I got off in the evenings, I could massage your legs and exercise them. I know you'd get stronger faster."

"You would marry me under these circumstances?" Alex asked, incredulous. "Oh, Bill, I do love you! But we don't know each other. Don't we need to get better acquainted before we think of taking such a giant step?"

"I know you. Say yes, Alex...and we'll be married right now," Bill pleaded.

"Right now, silly?" she asked, giggling. "It takes days! There's the blood test, the marriage license, and I would want a wedding dress." Alex was too excited to imagine how she would look being married in a wedding dress, sitting in a wheelchair.

"Speaking of wedding dresses," she continued, "what about my parents? Do you think they'll agree to my marrying you? Oh, gosh, I'm even afraid to ask them"

"You're over twenty-one, Alex," Bill reminded her. "You don't need their consent, but I'm sure you would want their blessing as much as I do. It's Ken Minard who bothers me. What will he say?"

"Ken and I are only good friends," Alex reassured Bill. "He will be overjoyed."

"Are you sure?" Bill persisted.

"Reasonably, but I'll call him and tell him the good news and see what he says," she promised.

"Okay, darling, but you need to rest for a while now." Bill left Alex in the care of the transporting nurse and went back to his other patients.

Alex couldn't rest; she had to tell Ken. She picked up the telephone and dialed his office number. Caroline Wells answered the phone and informed Alex that Ken was at the hospital.

"Ask one of the nurses to page him," she suggested.

"Thanks, I will," Alex said. She hung up and rang for a nurse. "Will you have Dr. Minard paged, please?" she asked when the woman appeared.

"Certainly, Miss Shaw."

It was only a few seconds until Alex heard his page over the intercom. Minutes later, Ken appeared in her room.

"What's so urgent, Miss Shaw?" he asked, acting quite the professional.

"Oh, Ken, I have the most wonderful news, and I couldn't wait another minute to tell you," Alex Ann bubbled.

"You took three steps today," Ken announced, thinking, *I beat her to the surprise this time.*

"Yes," she nodded, "I did that, but that's not all." She held her breath for several seconds, then almost shouted, "I'm getting married!"

"Married?" he asked, puzzled. "When?"

"Right away. Bill asked me yesterday, and we want to get married as soon as possible," Alex explained in a hurried voice. "He says he can set up a better therapy program and I'll be able to leave the hospital. Oh, Ken, say you're happy for me."

He held her in his arms for a moment, then said, "You know I am, Alex. I couldn't be more happier. I think it's great."

"I was sure you would think so, but I had to tell you first. Mother and Dad don't know yet," she admitted.

"Thanks for feeling that I was special. I wish both of you all the happiness in the world," Ken congratulated her.

"Well, now I have to tell Mother and Dad," she said, a bit of her exuberance fading. "Do you think they'll be difficult?"

"No, I'm sure they'll be as pleased as I am," Ken answered. "All they really want is your happiness. If you're happy with Bill, they'll be happy. It's that simple. I thought for a long time that there was something between you and Dr. Brant, so I'm really not surprised," Dr. Ken lied.

"I'm chicken," Alex admitted. "Would you stay until I tell them?" she pleaded. "They'll be here in a few minutes."

"Yes, dear, I'll stay, unless I'm called out on an emergency. Then, you realize, I'd have to leave," Ken replied.

"Yes, Dr. Minard," Alex teased. "I'm getting the hang of it already. It won't be easy being a doctor's wife."

"Well, Bill's type of specialty is a little less hectic than mine," Ken stated. "You see, you're getting the better guy, after all."

Just then, Sam and Mervice walked into Alexandria's room. They felt something was wrong because Ken was there.

"What's wrong, Alex?" Mervice asked anxiously. "Ken, has something happened to Alexandria's legs?"

"Nothing is wrong, Mrs. Shaw," Ken reassured her. "Something is right, all right, but I'll let Alex tell you."

"Oh, Mother...Daddy"I'm going to be married!" Alex burst out with her secret.

"Married!" Sam exclaimed. "In your condition?" He couldn't believe he'd heard her right.

"Yes, Daddy," Alex nodded. "Bill Brant has asked me to marry him, and I have accepted."

"Without even consulting us?" Mervice cried.

"I didn't have time to ask anyone. It all happened so quickly. I walked three steps that first day on the ramp, and when I began to get tired I fell forward. Bill caught me, and that's when we realized how much we had come to love each other," she explained. "If we're married, he can spend more time giving me therapy and I will get stronger sooner. Oh, Mother, say it's okay! Please, Daddy, say you're happy for me!" she begged.

Mervice was astonished. She had never suspected, through all the months that Alex was taking therapy, that a romantic relationship had developed between Alex and Dr. Bill Brant.

"Well, you'll have to give us some time to think about it," her mother answered evasively. "You must realize that it comes as a bit of a shock."

"How do you feel about this, Ken?" Sam asked his friend.

"I think it's great," Ken affirmed. "They're in love, and need each other. What else is life about? I think he's right about the therapy program. He'll be able to devote more time to Alex. Bill can bring her here as an out-patient for the rigid exercises, and during his hours off can do the massage himself."

"But, Alexandria, your lifestyle doesn't fit into the schedule of a doctor," Sam protested.

"I intend to make it fit, Daddy," Alex replied stubbornly. "I've learned a lot since I've been here about the wonderful work that people like Ken, Bill and Dr. Blanding are doing, not to mention Dr. Peters and Nurse Bell, who have worked hard with the patients on the neurological floor. If I'm able to walk again, I want to do something to try to repay them for all their efforts. I could do volunteer work, or maybe even become a therapist, like Bill."

The announcement didn't sound at all like Alex. It wouldn't be easy for someone as self-centered as Alex to change.

"What do you mean, *if* you walk again?" Bill Brant questioned, as he entered the room. "You'll walk again. I'll see to that."

"Well, good folks, I have work to do," Ken announced. "I'll see all of you later." Ken loped off, feeling the need to get out of the room and out of the middle of a controversy between parents and prospective son-in-law.

After Ken departed, Sam turned to Bill and said, "Alexandria says you've asked her to marry you, and she has accepted."

"That's right, Mr. Shaw," Bill nodded. "I love Alex Ann and want to marry her right away, but I would like to have your and Mrs. Shaw's approval," he added.

"Alexandria has been used to an entirely different lifestyle than the one you propose to offer her," Mervice objected. "Do you think she is emotionally capable of adjusting to a new lifestyle so different from the one she's used to?"

"Yes, I do," Bill replied firmly. "I believe Alex Ann is emotionally strong enough to do anything she wants. It'll take time and a lot of hard work before Alex can function normally. With the progress she's made so far, I feel certain she'll be able to accomplish it within a few months."

"Please, Mother and Daddy," Alex begged, "think about it! Will you at least do that for me?"

"We can get together later and discuss this further," Sam decided. "Dr, Brant, I expect to get another opinion about Alex before I give my consent to her marrying anyone."

"That's your privilege, Mr. Shaw," Bill conceded, "and I'll welcome any advice from whomever you choose to consult. You realize, though, that Dr. Peters is her neurologist. I'm only her therapist. By the way, Dr. Barkley will be home from Europe this weekend. He's a leader in his field, and I'm sure Dr. Peters will ask for his opinion."

"That's very nice of you, Dr. Brant," Mervice spoke up. "We'll talk later."

Bill realized it was a signal for him to leave the Shaw family alone to think about what was best for Alex. After all, she was the important one to be considered. She was the one who would have to fight to walk, and it might take longer than any of them could surmise.

CHAPTER 8

Autumn came to Pennsylvania with orange and golden forests, and the beginning of hunting season, one of the most avid sports in that great commonwealth. The amusement parks closed and school began.

On October fifth and eighth, the annual Steeplechase was held in Ligonier Valley at the beautiful country estate—Rolling Rock—owned by General Richard King Mellon. The proceeds of the race went to the hospital for Crippled Children in Pittsburgh, an institution near and dear to Ken Minard's heart.

Ken had never attended a steeplechase. It was for the elite of the city, and when Ken lived in Pittsburgh as a young man he didn't have access to that kind of money.

Caroline Wells was an avid steeplechase fan and had attended the Rolling Rock Races many times. She continually expatiated about Ligonier Valley and how beautiful it was.

"We just have to go to the races this year, Ken," she said enthusiastically. "You'll simply adore all those beautiful horses and hounds."

"Caroline, events such as that one are expensive, and you know quite well I have had a lot of expense what with the new equipment we installed and the fact that patients do not pay bills on time. My finances at the moment are really crippled."

"Oh, but you see...it's not expensive to go to the races," Caroline protested. "We could go only to the Saturday one, and the gate fee is ten dollars. By not staying over, the only other expense would be our gasoline out and back. We can take my little roadster, which wouldn't use as much fuel as your bigger car. Please, Ken," she pleaded, "will you at least consider it?"

"Aw. you know I can't refuse you anything," Ken replied helplessly. "Your exuberance could startle a turtle into running. All right, if I can arrange my schedule and Dr. John can cope by himself, we'll go to your beloved steeplechase."

"Have you ever been to Ligonier?" Caroline asked.

"No, I've never been that far east," Ken admitted. "I think I've been to Jeanette, but never Ligonier."

"Well, you're in for a real treat," Caroline laughed.

Since the office was closed on Saturdays, Ken needed a standby for the day at the hospital. He had stood by for Dr. Jack Zill for two weekends, so that was the first person Ken called.

"Jack?" Ken asked, when a man answered the telephone at the other end.

"Yes," the male voice replied. "Is this Ken? Hey, what's up?"

"Caroline insists that we attend the steeplechase at Rolling Rock this weekend," Ken replied immediately, "and I need a standby."

"Go to your races, man, and forget about medicine for the day," Jack replied at once. "I'll be glad to repay your kind favor."

"That's great," Ken said. "Thanks, Jack, and I'll get with you later on the details."

After he hung up, he thought, *Am I copping out? Would a dedicated doctor take the day off to go to a horse race?* Then he reminded himself: *All work and no play makes Ken a heart attack prospect.*

Saturday morning dawned as one of the most gorgeous fall days in Ken's recollection of Pennsylvania. They piled into

Caroline's little roadster, adding cameras, jackets, binoculars and a chest full of cold drinks.

They left downtown Pittsburgh, passed Forbes Field, The Carnegie Institute of Technology, went through the tunnel under Squirrel Hill, crossed the George Westinghouse Bridge and were on their happy way. The highway, Route 30, was four lanes all the way from Pittsburgh to Irwin and on to Greensburg.

Greensburg is the county seat of Westmoreland County and built on top of a hill. To get to and from that great city, in any direction, one either has to go up or down a hill. There are one-way streets everywhere, and Ken wasn't used to driving in the hilly country, so Caroline offered to drive from Greensburg to Ligonier. Ken agreed. He could be looking around and drinking in all the gorgeous sights as they sped along.

Westmoreland County is a large county, surrounded by Allegheny (Pittsburgh), Somerset (Somerset), and Cambria counties. Cambria County is the home of Johnstown, the famous "flood city" listed in elementary history books.

After they left Greensburg, they entered the rolling hills of Pennsylvania and soon came to Latrobe, the home of the world-famous golfer, Arnold Palmer. Ken was familiar with Latrobe for another reason. Patients had been brought into the Pittsburgh hospitals from the Latrobe Hospital because they lacked a special facility or machine.

After they passed Latrobe, they drove on to Longbridge, where they passed through a natural tunnel of trees grown so thick and bushy that they almost covered the highway. The leaves were brown, yellow and orange, and it was like driving through a fairyland of foliage.

Between the two lanes of the four-lane highway was the Loyalhanna Creek. It was low this time of year, and the big rocks were white and shiny, gleaming at the passersby. In some places the trees were so dense that the creek wasn't visible. After they crossed Longbridge, they came to the entrance to Idlewild Park.

"What's that?" Ken asked.

"That's an amusement park, owned by the McDonald family," Caroline explained. "People come for miles around to swim, dance and picnic here. They have mechanical rides and all kinds of entertainment."

"Could we go in for just half an hour?" Ken asked.

"I'm sorry, darling, but Idlewild closes in September and doesn't open again until May," Caroline announced.

"Shucks," Ken moaned as he settled back in the seat.

Ascending over the brow of a hill, Ken leaned forward in disbelief. "What's that?" he shouted.

"A castle," Caroline answered simply.

"A castle? Here in Ligonier Valley? Who would build a medieval castle here? It reminds me of merry old England," Ken decided.

"That's Storybook Forest, silly," Caroline laughed. "It's like a fairyland or Mother Goose Land. They show all kinds of fairy tales: Red Riding Hood, The Old Woman in the Shoe, Cinderella—and they are all acted out by live people dressed in the appropriate garb."

Before Ken could look twice, they had sped past and the fairytale castle was gone from sight.

"It sounds like a small Disney World," Ken said dreamily.

"Oh, that's where I'd like to go," Caroline exclaimed. "Will you take me to Disney World someday, Ken?"

"Yes, darling, when we get some time off, we'll go," he promised. He then wondered if he would ever have time to go home again, or how long it would be before he would visit Florida.

They passed a road sign that stated: "Ligonier, five miles."

"We're almost there," Caroline exclaimed.

"You were right when you said Ligonier Valley was beautiful—at least the little bit I've seen is unbelievable," Ken cried.

"It's called the 'Playground of Pennsylvania,' because there are so many exciting things to do and see," Caroline boasted.

"Like what?" Ken demanded good-naturedly.

"Like Fort Ligonier. You know they restored the fort some years ago and have a museum there. It looks like a real fort. We'll pass it directly, so keep looking to the left. In the French and Indian War it was known as the 'Key to the West.' It was the connecting fort between Fort Duquesne, now known as Fort Pitt, and Fort Bedford," Caroline explained.

"Then there's the beautiful Laurel Valley Country Club," she continued. "It was built by Arnold Palmer, and the PGA is played there every so many years."

"Where are *we* going?" Ken asked. "They don't hold the races right here in town, do they?"

"Of course not, silly," Caroline giggled. "The races are held at the Mellon Estate. It's near Laughlintown, and we'll be there in a few minutes. On your left is the Ligonier Valley Beach. It's a swimming pool and dance pavilion. All the young people go there in the summer. It's super!" Caroline exclaimed.

"What happens if somebody gets sick in this town and needs to be hospitalized?" Ken asked.

"Typical doctor—always on duty," Caroline said wryly. "Well, for your professional information, Ligonier has a hospital. It's not very big, but it serves the valley well. Serious cases are transferred to Latrobe Hospital, or to one of the Pittsburgh hospitals," she answered.

"We're coming to the little village of Laughlintown," she said, changing the subject. "There's a museum there that has been restored by a group of local citizens. It's called Compass Inn. It was used as a stopping point for stagecoaches when they traveled east and west through Westmoreland County from Fort Bedfort to Fort Ligonier and Fort Pitt," Caroline babbled. "Maybe we can stop and look around."

"Do you know everything about this place?" Ken teased. "You must come here often. Are you sure the races have been your only interest in Ligonier Valley?"

"Ah, now, would you be jealous if there was another reason?" Caroline asked, really wanting Ken to answer the question.

"No, I'm getting too old for that," he admitted. "I'm satisfied with you just as you are, all past forgotten."

Ken was almost thirty. He was one of the youngest men to serve in the Florida Senate, but was only ten years older than Caroline.

Caroline turned right onto a macadam road and announced, "We'll be at our destination in a few minutes."

The terrain on either side of the road consisted of rolling hills, and luxuriously-kept farmlands were visible as far as the eye could see—miles and miles of rich grassland for the famous horses that were raised on the mammoth estate.

"This countryside is enchanting," Ken observed. "It reminds me of the stories I've read about the English countryside where they have queen's hunts and everyone dresses up in red and black and rides a famous horse. Beautiful farmland," he murmured.

"It's not farmed, in the general sense," Caroline replied. "That is, it's used for raising horses and beef cattle. See the huge barns? Over there are the kennels for the hounds."

On a distant hill, they could see the beef cattle lowing back and forth over the grassy land. It was so quiet and still that Ken was lost for a few minutes in the soft surroundings.

"Hounds?" he finally questioned, surprised.

"Yes, they have a whole kennel of hunting hounds," she nodded. "They have an annual hunt just before the races begin each year. You said it reminded you of England. Well, it's just like that. You'll see the hounds just before the races start. The kennel master, on his shiny black stud, with red coat, black trousers and boots, will lead the hounds for the beginning of the race. After them, the horses and riders who are running in today's steeplechase will pass by the stands for all the spectators to see. It's so exciting," she cried.

They were approaching the gate, and Caroline had to slow down to present the tickets. The next big problem was a parking place. After that, they would go to the stands to await the sound of the trumpets for the annual Rolling Rock Steeplechase.

Ken was as excited as Caroline.

"I'm glad you know what you're doing and where you're going," he laughed. "I'd be lost in a minute, and you'd have to rescue me."

From the parking lot, Ken and Caroline walked for what seemed a mile, until they reached the stands. There were flocks of people everywhere, gathered together talking about the past races and the events of the day. Others were discussing the horses and possible winners. Of course, there were present the usual bands of young people, their blankets and soft drinks in hand.

From the stands, they watched the people milling about. Out over the terrain, they viewed the whole steeplechase course. The hedges were all freshly shaped and shorn for the exciting racing days. Off in the distance, they could see hills, backed by higher hills. From where they were, at the foot of the Laurel HIll Mountains, they could also see the peak of the Chestnut Ridge ten miles away. The view was breathtaking. Ken seemed stunned for a few minutes that he'd been fortunate enough to come to Ligonier Valley and Rolling Rock for the fascinating event.

They observed the crowd shifting back and forth. They were of all ages, from all walks of life, but most of all they were wealthy, with mink coats and fancy hats. The weather had warmed, so the coats would later have to be discarded. One could be sure that the attire underneath was an elegant as the coat.

The races went well. There were no serious accidents. The winner was taken to the circle and the proper flower collar was bestowed. Pictures were snapped and the race was officially over, at least for the spectators. There would follow all kinds of victory parties and inebriated ladies and gentlemen before the night was over.

After Ken and Caroline left the steeplechase grounds, and since they couldn't enter into any of the festivities, they drove to the top of Laurel Hill Mountain. The foliage was supernatural in all its autumn splendor. Ken wasn't used to being at such a high elevation, for Tampa was just a few feet above sea level.

"How resplendent," Ken remarked. "What a beautiful place for a mountain cabin. I could steal away on weekends in the summer and hide among this thick underbrush and be lost to humanity. All nature lives here."

As he spoke, a white-tailed deer passed over the highway in front of them. Caroline slowed to a near stop while three others followed the first. They dashed off into the forest.

"The wonders of nature are everywhere," Ken murmured, "in the sea, the sky, the mountains...."

"Your idea of a cabin is great," Caroline agreed, "but you could come out on weekends in the winter, too. The ski lodge isn't far from here and we could ski all we wanted."

"Snow ski?" Ken cried. "I'd break my bloody neck! I haven't skied for so many years I know I'd kill myself the first trip down."

"No, you wouldn't," Caroline laughed. "It all comes back. It's like riding a bicycle. You never forget how."

"Don't bet on it," Ken replied dryly, "but this is a day to dream, and dream we will." Ken put his arm around Caroline, kissed her lightly, and asked, "Where to next, my love? What other exciting revelations do you have in store?"

He knew that Caroline would fill the day as full as possible with all the goodies she could conjure up. Since it was so seldom they got a day off, she would do it all at one time.

"The Latrobe Airport," she replied immediately. "Let's take a plane and soar around over Latrobe and Ligonier, and see all the beautiful hillsides and colored leaves."

"Airplane!" Ken exclaimed. "You said this trip wouldn't be expensive! I'm with you, Miss Wells, Latrobe, here we come...."

The landscape was a kaleidoscope of colors. Ken had forgotten how different Pennsylvania was from the tropical parts of the United States. So rugged, so difficult in the winter, but so splendid in the autumn. He reached over and took Caroline's hand in his.

"It's so wonderful, darling," he whispered. "Thanks for bringing me to Ligonier, 'The Playground of Pennsylvania.'"

"You're welcome, doctor, but we'll come here many more times, I hope," Caroline replied, as the plane descended and landed on the runway of the airport.

As they drove west on Route 30 for their return to Pittsburgh, Ken reminded Caroline that he owned a home on beautiful Tampa Bay. In return for her tour of Ligonier Valley, he would show her the tropical peninsula of Florida as soon as they could get away for a week or so.

That would be a perfect honeymoon, he thought, *but there's too much to do now to think of that.*

Ken and Caroline arrived in Pittsburgh about midnight, tired but elated that the day had been so perfect from beginning to end.

Ken took Caroline home, parked her little roadster in the garage, then bid a fond good night, got in his own car and started for Thirty-Second Street and his bed, wondering how many times that night the telephone would ring. Yet medicine was his business now, and he loved it first and foremost.

Quinter and Dr. Blanding had already retired when Ken quietly entered his room in the big brownstone house. It seemed that Dr. John retired earlier each night. Ken felt it was an indication his old friend was failing faster. However, it could also be that Dr. John was merely being cautious by resting more. Ken undressed and got into bed, tired but exhilarated after the most perfect and enjoyable day of his life.

When Ken came down to breakfast the next morning, he noticed that Quinter looked slightly downcast.

"What's the matter, Quinter?" Ken asked. "Is Dr. John all right?"

"He doesn't say much," Quinter answered, "but I feel as if there's something he's not telling us. What could it be, Dr. Ken? Could he be worse, and is hiding it from us?"

"It's possible, Quinter," Ken admitted. "I'll see if I can get him to discuss it with me. He may need to confide in someone and be hesitant to ask me to take on added responsibility. Thanks for the delicious breakfast," he added.

"Did you have a nice holiday yesterday?" Quinter asked.

"It was the most beautiful day of my life," Ken grinned. "Ligonier Valley really is all that Caroline said it would be."

"Yes, sir, it is that, all right," Quinter agreed. "Scores of city folks go there for the summer, and they all say the same thing."

Ken left the house to make hospital rounds, check on Alex Ann and then attend church at the large Church of the Brethren on Beechwood Boulevard. He had been able to attend church only a couple of times since arriving in Pittsburgh, and he usually went to the one nearest the hospital or office.

As he drove to the eleven a.m. service he wondered if Caroline attended church—if so, what church? Was she of the same faith as he? He'd never thought to ask her about her religious affiliations.

The one thing that Ken was grateful for, in coming from Tampa to Pittsburgh, was that both cities had the church of his choice. Suppose it wasn't Caroline's church.

"I'll think about that when the time comes," he murmured to himself.

Inside the church, Ken always sat in the back row, so that if he was called out, he could leave without disturbing anyone. He spoke to the usher and was just ready to sit down when a female voice spoke behind him.

"Good morning, Dr. Minard."

Ken turned around and was astonished to see Christine Wells standing behind him.

"I didn't know you were a Brethren," she smiled.

"Good morning, Mrs. Wells," Ken replied with a slight bow. "Yes, I'm Brethren, and have been most of my adult life. I'm overjoyed to know we share the same faith. Is Caroline here?"

Ken had not been a member of any church, had not been baptized and hadn't even considered joining a church until after he was drafted into the armed forces. He found Christ on a remote island in the South Pacific.

When he came back to the United States, while in medical school, he attended whatever church he could. Then one day the pastor of a small congregation came to Ken's office for medical attention. Through him, Ken decided to join the Church of the Brethren. It meant he would have to be baptized by triune immersion—that is, he would be put under water three times forward, in the name of the Father, the Son, and the Holy Spirit.It was the most moving experience of Ken's entire life, and he had been a devout Brethren since, giving the church as much of his time as he possibly could.

"Caroline sings in the choir," Mrs. Wells explained. "This morning she is going to sing the solo and descant."

"How perfect," Ken replied. "Maybe I'll see you later today. I must sit in the back pew, so I'm available if needed," he explained.

What a devout young man, Mrs. Wells thought. *He's more interested in the church, it seems, than is Caroline. Then, he's older, too,* she decided, then wandered down the aisle to join her husband.

After she left, Ken thought, *She came in late and was carrying books and papers. She's probably a teacher. I wonder what age group she teaches.*

The services began and when Caroline stood to sing, Ken was overjoyed. He was so happy to know they were members of the same church. She'd never told Ken she could sing. It was then he realized that there were probably many things he didn't know about Caroline, and vice versa. It takes years to know someone, if it is ever possible to really know anybody.

Just before the end of the sermon, an usher tapped Ken on the shoulder, and said, "There's a call for you, Doctor. You can take it in the pastor's study."

Ken slipped out quietly and answered the phone. It was Quinter.

"Could you come quickly, sir?" he asked.

"I'll be right there," Ken promised. "Is it Dr. John?"

"Yes, sir, he's very ill," Quinter answered.

Ken sped home as fast as he could without breaking too many laws, thinking all the time, *Has the time come? Is this the end? Are we going to lose Dr. John?*

When Ken got up to leave, Caroline recognized him and her heart leaped. *He came to hear me sing,* she thought. *But how did he know? Mother...she's been conspiring against me!*

When church was over, Caroline hung up her choir robe and dashed up the back steps to the car. Her parents were waiting.

"You told Ken I was singing today, didn't you?" she accused her mother. "Oh, Mother, how could you? Without even telling me?"

"I told Dr. Minard nothing, Caroline," Christine replied firmly. "I saw him when he came into church. He's a member of our church, but he doesn't get to attend very often. You, of all people, should understand why."

"Oh, how wonderful!" Caroline cried. "We go to the same church. You know, Mother, I never thought to ask Ken about his religious beliefs."

"Shame on you, Caroline," her mother chided gently. "I thought that would be one of the first things you would have inquired into. Then, you young people aren't as conscientious as we were at your age."

"That's not fair, Mother," Caroline protested. "I'm considerate of my church. I just had so many other things to think about."

Caroline was glad when the conversation ended.

CHAPTER 9

At first, Ken thought Quinter might be exaggerating Dr. John's condition. His treatments had been making him very ill, but it usually lasted for three or four days, then subsided.

Ken parked the car, flew in the back door and up the stairs to Dr. John's bedroom. His friend lay on the bed, pale and weak, hardly able to talk.

"What is is, Dr. John?" Ken begged. "What do you want from me. I'll do anything."

"I'm hemorrhaging from the intestinal area. I'm afraid it will mean surgery. I'm not sure it would do any good to go through with it, but my heart is good, I think, and it may prolong my life by a few months. Would you take me to the hospital, Ken? I'm so weak."

"I'll do whatever you suggest, Dr. John," Ken promised, "but you must go in an ambulance. I'll call one right now and go with you. I can catch a ride back, or Quinter can pick me up later."

Ken telephoned for an ambulance and took Dr. John to West End Hospital. He felt so forlorn as they wheeled the doctor into his room and transferred him onto a hospital bed.

Ken prayed each step of the way.

"We're not ready, God. We still need him. Spare him just a few more months, although, of course, we'll abide by your decision. If you need him now, give us the strength and grace to give him up."

"Which surgeon do you want to consult?" Ken asked his friend.

It was Sunday, and no doctors were available at that point. Ken felt it might be an emergency. He and Dr. John agreed to call Dr. Ben Luther at his home. Ken placed the call.

"Dr. Luther, this is Dr. Ken Minard. I'm sorry to bother you at home on Sunday, but I'm at West End with Dr. John Blanding. He's hemorrhaging from the bowel and asked that you be consulted," Ken explained quickly.

"I'll be there in a few minutes," Dr. Luther said at once and hung up.

Dr. Ben Luther was the son of a doctor and the grandson of a doctor, and all three had practiced at the Pittsburgh hospitals. Dr. Ben wasn't sure he was cut out for a medical career, but his father kept insisting that he consider it. Like Ken Minard, after his hitch in the service, he decided to give it a try. He specialized because he thought his life would not be as hectic as the general practitioner; he found he was mistaken. Surgeons had emergencies, the same as general practitioners. However, medicine had become his life. He felt a slight tremor of worry as he was called upon to treat one of the most dedicated men in all the history of the Pittsburgh hospitals.

Dr. Blanding had no children, as Dr. Luther knew. His wife had been unable to bear children, and they put off adopting until it was too late. Laura Blanding died of a malignancy, when she was forty-seven years old, and Dr. John never remarried. He had partially adopted Ken and was so proud of Ken's role in medicine.

When Ken approached Dr. John about leaving medicine and becoming a senator, Dr. John replied, "You are a born doctor. You'll be wasting your time, but I can't tell you what to do; you must decide for yourself."

He'd been highly disappointed when Ken chose to run for political office. He knew Ken couldn't stay away from medicine for long and felt his illness had created the opportune time to persuade Ken to return to the medical profession.

When Ken accepted his call the previous February, Dr. John was overjoyed. From then on, he worked with Ken and the hospitals to help him get established. When his time came, Dr. John knew he could pass on to meet Laura, his only real love, besides medicine, with a clear conscience that he was leaving his patients in the best possible hands.

Twenty minutes later, Dr. Luther arrived at the hospital room of Dr. John Blanding, his medical idol, and said, "Good afternoon, Doctor. What is it that I can do for you?"

"I'm hemorrhaging, and I think surgery is the only answer. I've been X-rayed, and re-X-rayed, so it won't be necessary to do any more of that. They're all available for your opinion in the necessary departments. I'm losing ground fast," Dr. John admitted. "I've been taking some treatments, but to no avail."

Dr. Luther read the X-rays and decided to operate if all the other tests were in order. Dr. John's complete medical history was made available, and Dr. Luther decided to operate within the next two hours. He went back to Dr. John's room, gave him the results, and asked for his permission to operate.

"As soon as you're ready, Dr. Luther," Dr. John stated. "I feel the sooner, the better. I'm sorry to spoil your Sunday, though. I know you relish a day off just as much as the rest of us do," Dr. John apologized.

"Don't worry about it, Dr. John," the other man shrugged it off. "How many Sundays have you given up in your short career as one of the leading general practitioners in this town? You even delivered babies for thirty years, didn't you?"

"You bet I did, night and day, Sunday, every day," Dr. John admitted. "Babies don't wait for Monday morning. Obstetrics is a hard life, but so rewarding. There is no greater satisfaction than to see a tiny, new baby breathe for the first time," Dr. John reminisced.

"You're right, except to see a man keep on living after you've opened him, removed part of him and sewed him back together. That's what I'm about to do with you," Dr. Luther stated.

"Let's go, then, and pray that I'll be spared a few more months to finish my task," Dr. John replied tiredly.

"You have a brilliant young man working with you," Dr. Luther said. "I hear good things about him all the time."

"Yes, Ben, he's really something. Came here and took hold right away. A young, strong and invigorating man. He'll make out, of that I'm sure," Dr. John boasted weakly.

The operation was a success. Dr. Luther removed a portion of the intestine and felt, with some treatments, Dr. John would be back on his feet in six weeks. His time was short—three months, six months. Who could possibly guess where cancer was concerned? The patient's attitude made a big difference in the recovery.

When Dr. Blanding awoke, Ken was standing beside the bed.

"Am I still in one piece?" the old doctor mumbled.

"Well, you're missing a few feet of intestine, but that's all," Ken replied thoughtfully. "It went well. You'll need some treatments, and Dr. Luther will be by later to explain everything. You must rest now and be a good patient. Remember, no bossing the nurses," Ken directed in a kidding manner. "You're the patient now, not the doctor."

"I was hoping that would never happen, but we're all dispensable. Remember that, Ken, and don't drive yourself too hard. It doesn't pay."

"I'll remember," Ken promised. "Now, you rest, and I'll look in on you again before I go to bed. Is there anything special I can do for you?" Ken asked.

"Be a good doctor is all I ask," Dr. John replied.

Dr. John would sleep and wake up several times for the next few hours. Ken had made arrangements for private duty nurses around the clock. The first one had arrived, so Ken felt free to leave and go home for a while.

Dr. Blanding spent twelve days in the hospital. He was then released with the provision that he had nursing care at home. Dr. Luther commanded him to do as he was told, but it was hard for Dr. John to rest and be quiet when there was still so much to be done.

At the end of the third week, he was feeling much better, and decided he was capable of doing some extra work on the patient files.

The first day Ken set aside one hour to go over the files with Dr. John and make himself familiar with each case. He realized that even one hour was too long for Dr. John to work without rest. Time was short, and knowing that Dr. John had common sense, as well as expert professional ability, Ken worked as long as Dr. John asked of him.

Dr. John's patients were mostly middle-income families, but he also had some very underprivileged ones and a small percentage from the higher income bracket. He seemed to consider it more of a privilege to work with the poor people. His ultimate humility and devotion were incomprehensible.

Although he'd stopped his obstectrical practice years before, he was still seeing patients he'd delivered ten or twelve years earlier.

"Nothing makes you feel older than to see a patient that you delivered; a six-pound-nine-ounce baby, looking you square in the eye," Dr. John said, half boasting, half reminiscing.

He discussed many things about his patients—their emotional hang-ups, their religious beliefs, their successes, and failures, their likes and dislikes. It all took time, and they covered such a little bit of territory each day.

Will we ever get through these files? Ken wondered. *They seem endless.*

Dr. John was not back on his feet in six weeks, as Dr. Luther had contemplated. He continued treatments and they were so severe that he was almost incapacitated for two or three days at a time. He was beginning to lose his grip on things, which was unusual for Dr. John. He was becoming disinterested in everything but medicine. It was his whole life now.

Dr. Luther suggested he take care of any legal matters necessary to settling his estate.

"How long do I have?" Dr. John asked.

"Three to six months, Dr. John," the prominent surgeon replied honestly. "More, if we can perform a miracle. The cancer has moved to other areas, and it will be only a matter of time until it affects a major organ. We'll fight it as long as we can. Of course, we'll pray," he added.

"Thanks, Ben. I believe prayer will be the best answer in my case—not to be healed, but for the grace and peace to leave this world bravely and not bitterly. I appreciate your help and brilliant knowledge where my physical body is concerned. Now, I'll dwell on the spiritual body and see if I can perfect it a little before I call it quits," Dr. John decided.

Some days, Dr. John felt fairly well, then in another few days, he'd be completely exhausted.

Ken went over many of the files with Mary Ann or Caroline. They were self-explanatory. If it wasn't an unusual case, Ken made mental notes about them. That left only the difficult cases for Dr. John's explanation.

The days wore on, and Dr. John Blanding failed a little more each day. It would soon be Thanksgiving, and then Christmas.

Will I be here until Christmas? Dr. John asked himself. His seventy-fifth birthday fell between Christmas and New Years. *Will I see that day? By living one day at a time, I just might make it.*

Mervice Shaw had been in Pittsburgh since the preceding spring. She was desperately hoping they could take Alexandria home for Thanksgiving and Christmas holidays.

Sam had commuted back and forth from Tampa, and the expense was becoming astronomical. Mervice longed for her own home, her own things and the nicer weather of Tampa. The cold was beginning to invade Pittsburgh. Mervice was tired of hospitals, the smell of medicine and conversations with sick people. She needed to get back into the activities of a Senator's wife, and she was sure Sam felt the same way.

Now Alexandria wanted to get married. Mervice was afraid it was only a flirtation, like before, that would pass once her daughter was well and could get back to her old way of life. She talked with Alex Ann and tried to convince her of this, but had gotten nowhere.

A wedding in a wheelchair. How grotesque! Not their Alexandria! Mervice couldn't conceive such a thing. They would have to wait until she was well, then she could have a beautiful wedding in Tampa.

If she was able to leave the hospital, they could take her home and she could be treated as an outpatient at a Tampa hospital. Tampa had good physical therapists. Mervice was determined to talk with Sam when he returned to Pittsburgh over the weekend. She was going to convince him that it was the best plan for everyone involved.

On Saturday morning, Sam and Mervice went to visit Alex Ann. They were going to try to persuade her to give up her marriage plans, go home to Tampa, and have treatments there as an outpatient.

Alex Ann was being torn apart. She wanted so much to be with Bill, but she was so homesick. The weather would be nice, sunny and pleasant.

"Oh, Daddy, I want to go home," Alex Ann admitted, "really I do! But I can't leave Bill. I must stay and keep up with my treatments. Besides, I need him so."

"Bill can fly down over the weekends to be with you for the holidays," Sam suggested. "You can have your therapy right there in Tampa. Mother is tired and we need to get home and settled before the Yule and New Year's parties begin. Mother has so many things she must do."

"I'm not sure Bill has the finances to fly all over the continent, but you make it sound so easy and inviting," Alex Ann admitted.

"If you find out that things don't work as you planned, you can come back here and resume your therapy program," Sam persisted. "Will you consider going home, Alex, at least for your mother's sake?"

"I'll think about it," she promised, "but I'm not sure the doctors will agree with you. They may not want to release me. Oh, to be home for Christmas," she sighed. "How wonderful!

It's such a small thing, but to me, it's everything. Some of the things I valued so highly a year ago mean nothing to me now. If I could just learn to walk, if my legs would just hold me and I could step by myself, that would be all the Christmas I need."

"Then you'll go?" Mervice asked.

"I'll talk to Dr. Peters and Bill about it when they make rounds today. What if they say I can't? You'll let me come back, if necessary, won't you? Promise me that before I ask," she pleaded.

"Yes, of course," Sam promised. "If they suggest it, we will certainly consider it."

When Dr. Peters made rounds that morning, Alex discussed the plans with him.

"Do *you* want to go home, Alexandria?" he inquired.

"Yes, very much, Doctor," she nodded, "at least for the holidays. Could we make arrangements for a therapy program in Tampa?"

"We'll contact the hospital and see," he stated. "I see no reason why they wouldn't be able to carry on with the program we've begun here. Have you discussed this with Dr. Brant? I understand you two have become emotionally involved."

"No, I haven't talked with him yet," she admitted. "He wants to get married right away, but I'm hesitant about rushing into something I might later regret. I'd like to go home for the holidays, and maybe he could spend Christmas with me. That would give us a chance to decide how we really feel about each other."

"You're a very wise young lady," Dr. Peters commended. "That sounds like an excellent idea."

"When Bill has some free time, I'll discuss the plans with him, tell him you have given permission, and see what his reaction will be."

"Very well, Miss Shaw. Then I'll get together with Dr. Brant on a professional level and see if he thinks it advisable. When you decide, notify me and I'll make arrangements with the Tampa hospital to continue your treatments. This may be just what you need," he added.

When Nurse Bell came to take Alex to therapy that afternoon, she was shocked to find that Alex wasn't going.

"Would you ask Dr. Brant to come here, please?" Alex asked. "I need to talk to him."

"Of course, Miss Shaw," Nurse Bell nodded, "but are you sure you want to miss your therapy time? It's so important."

"We'll see, after I talk with Dr. Brant," Alex replied. "I may be going home. Won't that be great?" Alex exclaimed.

"Yes, Alex, that'll be great, going home for Christmas...." the nurse replied wistfully. "I'll have to work Christmas. We have small parties here and have a little fun, but it's not the same as being at home with the children. Children were made for Christmas; after all, it is a child's birthday. The birthday of the King."

"Yes, there's no other holiday or birthday to compare with Christmas," Alex agreed. "I hope you get the day off, Mrs. Bell, and can spend it with your family. I also hope things work out so I can go home. I can't believe it! Last year at this time, I was healthy and so alive. If I'd known my life would take such a drastic turn, I wouldn't have wanted to live. I've learned so much from my illness. I guess God has a reason for the things he does. 'All things happen for good to those who love God,' or some such statement," Alex noted. "My, I didn't realize how far away from God I had gotten until now. I've been so selfish and overbearing. Do you suppose God will forgive me, Mrs. Bell?" Alex asked.

"Yes, Alex Ann, God will forgive you if you sincerely ask Him, and if you lean on Him it will be easier for you. Now, I'll go and call Dr. Brant. He'll wonder what has happened to us."

"Thank you, Nurse Bell, for everything," Alex said with sincerity. "Your patience and kindness are overwhelming. Not all the nurses take time to listen, nor do they have your compassion." Tears slipped down the young girl's cheeks.

Nurse Bell went to summon Bill, and Alex began to have second thoughts about going home.

I can come back if things don't work out, but how can I leave Bill? I'll miss seeing him every day.

Bill Brant was disappointed that Alex didn't come for therapy. When he entered her room, she was still crying.

"What's wrong, Alex, darling?" he cried, gathering her into his arms. "Are you sick? You haven't fallen again, have you?"

"I'm sorry, sweetheart," Alex sobbed. "No, I'm all right. I wanted to use my therapy time to discuss something with you. What would you say if I went home for the holidays?" she asked in a small voice.

"Would you come back?" he questioned.

"I don't know. We'll see about that when the time comes. Dr. Peters has given his permission, but I need yours, too, and not just your medical permission."

"What about your therapy program? What about our plans?" Bill's heart felt as if it would crack.

"Dr. Peters is going to call the Tampa hospital and see if I could have therapy there as an outpatient. I could live at home, and Daddy and Mother would care for me. You could come for the holidays...and, oh, we'd have such fun!"

Bill was stricken. He was sure he'd never see Alexandria again. All of his old insecurities came to light again. It was a tremendous challenge when Bill was assigned to Alex's case. If he could help her walk again, he would realize his dream. He hadn't counted on falling in love with her.

Tampa was twelve hundred miles away. Alex was a senator's daughter, and entirely out of his league. He felt sure he wouldn't be able to get time off to go anywhere, much less Tampa, Florida. But Alex was entitled to go home if she could. It might do her more good emotionally and that was a necessary factor in Alex's recovery. How could he tell her he didn't want her to go? He had no choice; he must let her go.

"I won't be able to get off for the holidays," he said, "and I was counting on being with you during these precious days. That's no reason for you to stay, though. I'll make all the arrangements, if you like."

"I won't go if you can't get Christmas off," Alex replied stubbornly. "I'll stay here. Mother and Daddy can go home without me."

"No, Alex, I don't want that," Bill replied. "Your folks are entitled to their only daughter on Christmas. Besides, I think it would be good for you...the change, I mean."

"I can't leave you, Bill," Alex moaned. "It would spoil it all for me. Christmas wouldn't mean a thing without you."

"Maybe I could get two days off," Bill decided. "Maybe one of the other therapists would work that day for me and the day after. We don't do much on Christmas Day, so that would give me seventy-two hours to fly down and back. I want you to go home, Alex. I'll try to fix my schedule so I can be with you for a couple of days, okay?"

"Oh, that's wonderful!" Alex cried.

"Now, don't get up your hopes," he cautioned. "I may not be able to swing it. Dr. Peters may not be able to set up a satisfactory program for you in Tampa. When do your parents want to leave?"

"As soon as possible," she replied, "so we can be home for Thanksgiving as well. They have promised me that if it doesn't work out I can come back. And they'll keep their promise."

"You really want to go home, don't you, Alex?"

"Oh, yes, darling, I want to go home," Alex replied fervently.

"Then it's settled. We'll go ahead and make the arrangements," Bill decided firmly.

When Bill left the room, his heart jumped unnaturally. *If I let her go,* he thought, *I will never see her again. But I can't keep her here, I must let her go home for Christmas. She won't come back once she's there and settled. The weather will get cold here, and it's so nice there. I guess I'm being selfish, but I love her so, how can I let her go?*

For the balance of the afternoon, Bill was like a mannequin. He didn't talk any more than he had to, and he wasn't paying enough attention to his patients.

I must let her go, he decided. *I have no right to keep her here. I'm going to make her think all will be well between us if she leaves. I must be convincing, but how can I give her up? I'll lose her if I let her go.*

Bill forced his mind back to his work. Every patient was important. It was just that he loved Alexandria so much.

CHAPTER 10

The arrangements were made. The Shaws would go home for the holidays. Alex Ann would be able to get treatments in Tampa and live at home. She was ecstatic.

"I can't wait!" she cried. "I know it will be painful for me...the trip home, that is...but I'll just grit my teeth and think about something else."

"We'll give you an injection before you leave for the airport. That will help ease the pain a little," Dr. Peters promised. "You'll be all right, I'm sure."

"I hate to leave Bill," she said unhappily. "I'll miss him so. He'll miss me, too, more than he lets on."

"Dr. Brant will be all right. You just put your mind at ease and concentrate on your trip," Dr. Peters directed. "That is the most important thing now. I'll leave orders at the desk, some instructions for the hospital, and your file. You'll need to take those things with you. You'll walk again, Miss Shaw, if you try hard enough. I'll say good-bye now, and wish you all the success and happiness for the New Year."

"Thank you, Dr. Peters," Alex said. "I'll surely remember you as long as I live. I'll write you of my progress...and thanks again, for everything."

Alex Ann felt let down when Dr. Peters left. It was as if one of the spokes in a wheel had been broken or lost. She felt sure that as soon as they were on their way she would feel better.

The afternoon before their departure, Alex talked with her mother.

"Could I see Dr. Blanding before I leave? He's had surgery, and I'm sure he's not able to come here. I could go in a wheelchair. I think I could sit up long enough for a short visit. Will someone take me?"

"We'll see, Alexandria," Mervice said hesitantly. "That's a good bit to ask of anyone. Ken or Dr. Brant might take you if either had some free time."

"Will you ask one of them?" Alex persisted. "Ken would be the likely candidate. I'm sure he could arrange it."

Mervice Shaw was thoroughly disgusted. Why all the fuss about Dr. Blanding? They were ready to leave for Florida the following day, and Alex wanted to ride across town. Why couldn't she just write him a note, or give him a message through Dr. Minard?

Mervice was sure things would be different when they got home, and Alex was at last adjusted. She'd forget all these doctors and make new friends in Tampa. Her old friends would probably all snub her since she was a cripple. Nevertheless, Mervice was certain everything would be resolved once they were on their way.

Alexandria suspected her mother would not ask one of the men to take her to see Dr. Blanding, so she decided to act on her own. She picked up the telephone receiver and dialed Ken's office.

Caroline answered the phone, and Alex asked, "Is Dr. Minard there? This is Alexandria Shaw."

"Yes, he is, but he's with a patient," Caroline explained. "Could I take a message and have the doctor call you back?"

"Yes, please. I'm in Room 307 at West End. Would you have Dr. Minard call me back before lunch?" Alex asked.

"Yes, of course," Caroline replied. "You know, I've heard a lot about you, Miss Shaw. I'm Caroline Wells, Dr. Minard's secretary."

"Yes, Miss Wells, he speaks of you often, too," Alex replied in a friendly voice. "I'm really glad for both of you. He's a wonderful person. Since we're both friends of a friend, could you dispense with the Miss and just call me Alex Ann?"

"I sure will, if you'll call me Caroline."

"Thanks, Caroline," Alex said. "I called Ken because I want to come and see Dr. Blanding before I go home. Do you suppose I would be imposing if I asked Ken to come for me?" Alex suggested tentatively.

"Of course not," Caroline reassured her. "He'd be delighted. When did you want to come?"

"This afternoon, if possible."

"His appointment book is filled for this afternoon. Let me make a suggestion. I've been wanting to meet you, so why don't you wait until early evening, after we've both eaten. Then I'll come with Ken, and we can all come back to Dr. Blanding's house. That way, you and I can get acquainted, too."

"That's a great idea," Alex agreed enthusiastically. "Do you suppose it would be appropriate for me to invite Dr. Brant along? I'd like to spend as much of the evening with him as I could."

"That's a wonderful suggestion," Caroline replied. "I'll call Dr. Blanding and make sure it's all right, then I'll call you back. We'll pick you up about seven. Dr. Brant and Dr. Ken can carry your wheelchair up the steps with you in it. How's that for service?"

"Splendid." Alex laughed. "Thank you, Caroline. I'm looking forward to this evening."

After she hung up, Alex wondered if she'd jumped to conclusions. Perhaps Bill wouldn't be free to go. She should have asked first, before making any plans. What about her parents? They'd be coming to visit about that time. Oh, well, she would be spending all her time with them in Tampa. They wouldn't mind her going out one last evening in Pittsburgh.

She wanted more than anything to spend her last evening with Dr. Blanding. She wanted to thank him for all his kindnesses and help during her illness. He was the one who had introduced her to Dr. Peters, which had started her on the road to recovery.

Alex Ann wasn't prepared for the sight when she saw Dr. Blanding. He was thin and white, so much weaker than when she'd last seen him, and she couldn't help but think of the hopeless weeks that lay ahead for him. She tried not to show her concern when Ken and Bill carried her up the steps of the Blanding house to the second floor.

"Good evening, Miss Shaw," the elderly man greeted her jovially. "How nice of you to want to visit an old man on your last evening in our big city."

"But, you see...Doctor...I had an ulterior motive. This was the only way I could get the attention of my two favorite men."

Ken wheeled Alex into the spacious living room of the Blanding home. There was a massive fieldstone fireplace on the north wall, with a rounded hearth, extending from wall to wall. The ceilings were nine feet high, and they had been recently painted a pale buff color. The walls were papered with stripes of reds and greens and the same buff tone. It seemed as though, even if she stood on Ken's shoulders, she wouldn't be able to touch the ceiling. The furniture was old, but well kept. It was perfectly placed so that Alex's wheelchair could be maneuvered around.

Quinter was quite a handyman in the house. He did everything from gardening to cooking. He appeared, as from nowhere, and Ken introduced him to Alex and Bill.

"Would you care for some coffee?" he asked politely. "I could have it here in a few minutes."

"Yes, Quinter, let's all have a cup," Dr. John stated. "Now, tell me, Miss Shaw, how are you, really? Are you excited about going home?"

"Yes, Dr. Blanding, I'm very excited about going home," Alex admitted truthfully. "I'll miss Bill and, of course, Ken. Ken's been a member of our family for a long time. I hope that Bill will become a member in the future." She squeezed Bill's hand as she spoke, and a rapture went through him.

"Is she doing as she's told, Dr. Brant?" Dr. John kidded.

"Yes, sir, Alexandria is a very good patient," Bill nodded. "I'll miss her more than she can imagine. I hope to spend Christmas with her in Tampa. That is, if I can juggle my time around and fit it into my schedule."

"That's nice. I hope all your plans work out," the old doctor smiled. "I think I should tell you what a wonderful job Ken is doing here, Miss Shaw."

"Excuse me, sir, but couldn't you call me Alex Ann?" she interrupted. "Miss Shaw sounds much too formal."

"All right," he agreed, "if you'll call me Dr. John."

"Fair enough." Alex laughed. "I'm so proud of the way Ken has taken hold here, and I'm sure you appreciate everything he's done. We'll really miss him in Tampa."

"Are your legs getting stronger?" Dr. John asked. "Can you walk yet?"

"My legs are still quite weak, and I've taken only three or four steps. Everyone has hope, though, including myself. I have faith that I'll walk again," she announced with finality.

"That's what it takes. Work and faith," Dr. John nodded. "One without the other is useless. You must work harder every day, and have faith that each day will bring you closer to health and strength."

"What about you, Dr. John?" she questioned. She could see the weakness and strain that the man exhibited as he talked.

"My case is hopeless as far as medicine is concerned," he replied tiredly. "Three or four months is all I have, unless I find a miracle stored away somewhere. I've lived my life, though, and you're just beginning yours."

Alex's heart ached. The Dr. Johns of the world should never die. They should become immortal.

Coffee was served and with it some cakes that Quinter had baked the day before. They were delicious. Alex hated the thought of leaving all her new-found friends. She was fascinated by their humble hospitality.

Why can't we all live like this? she wondered. *No pomp, no ceremony. Being wealthy isn't everything. It sometimes takes away one's humility, and I'm beginning to find out how important that is. Dr. John must have money. He's been a doctor for many, many years, but he still lives as if he is just beginning practice. How I admire him, and would like to capture this trait.*

Alex could see that Dr. John was beginning to tire. They had been there long enough. The injection that Alex received before she left the hospital was beginning to wear off.

Dr. Brant was aware of it and suggested, "I think Alex has been out of bed long enough. We should take her back and let her rest as much as possible before the long trip home."

"Thank you for coming to visit," Dr. John said. "I don't have much company any more, especially pretty young ladies. Keep your chin up and try hard, Alex. You'll walk again. Now, if you'll excuse me, I won't go downstairs with you. Good-bye and God bless you."

"Good-bye, Dr. John," she called. "Bless you for all the wonderful things you've done for me, and for all the patients in the years past who would have died without your care. You are truly one of a kind."

"Thank you for your kind words. It makes life a little easier to bear when you know you've helped others a little and are not passing from this earth without some contribution to mankind."

When Alex was back in bed in the hospital, she made a vow: *I will walk again. For Dr. John, I will walk again.*

Bill spent the balance of the evening with Alex, and when visiting hours were over, they clung to each other in desperation, never wanting to be separated.

"I'll see if I can get off to go with you to the airport," Bill promised. "It'll be so hard to let you go, but I know I must," Bill sighed.

"Would you rather say good-bye here, and not come with me to the airport?" Alex suggested.

"No, I want to be with you as long as I can," he said, shaking his head. "It's almost two months until Christmas and those weeks will drag by slowly enough. Please, let me come with you," Bill pleaded.

"All right," Alex sobbed, "but I may make a scene. I'm not used to this sort of thing, and I really will hate leaving you. I wish you could come along and live in Tampa near me."

"That's impossible. My job is here, and I must make a living at what I know."

"I know that, and I'll try to be brave, but don't be surprised if I break down," Alex murmured.

"Good night, my love. I'll see you tomorrow," Bill vowed. "Try to rest, Alex. The trip will be hard for you."

"I will, my darling. Until tomorrow," Alex said, then thought, *...and tomorrow and tomorrow. How long will we be separated? Will Bill be able to come to Tampa for Christmas? I'll have to live one day at a time and pray that things will work out.*

Neither Alexandria Shaw nor Bill Brant slept very well that night.

The plane was to embark at two-forty p.m. Alex was packed and her mother and father were carrying packages and luggage to Bill's car. He would take them to the airport.

"It is simply amazing how much you have accumulated since you came here, Alexandria," Mervice complained. "Will we need to take all these things? We'll have to leave the plants and flowers here. Is there anyone in particular that you want to give them to?" she asked.

"Yes," Alex replied immediately,.."there's a lady five doors down, on the right side of the hall. She's an invalid and I want her to have them. She has very little company, and is so lonely. Maybe they will cheer her up a little," Alex decided.

"I'll be glad to get you out of here," Mervice almost snapped, "and away from these depressing sick people. I think it will be better for you."

You don't understand, Mother, Alex thought to herself. *I hate leaving the security of the hospital and the doctors. It'll be lonely at home. Here, I have the nurses, doctors and cleaning ladies. At home, there will be only you and Dad.*

There would also be the excitement of Thanksgiving, Christmas and the New Year. Surely her friends would drop in to see her once in a while.

When they got to the Greater Pittsburgh Airport, they discovered that the plane would be late. Bill was upset, for he was interested in getting Alex on the plane and home as quickly as possible. Medication lasted only so long, and it was important that Alex be on her way.

They went to the coffee shop. Mervice and Sam left Alex and Bill alone for the duration of the wait. They talked of many things and discussed how little they knew about each other.

Alex began to wish she'd stayed in her safe hospital room, in the secure surroundings of the nurses and doctors. At that moment, the plane was announced over the loudspeaker. Bill would help Sam load Alex on the plane and then he would be gone...maybe forever...from her.

She found herself beginning to feel let down. She must not. She would have to be brave for Bill's sake.

She was on the plane, the good-byes had been said, and Bill was gone.

Please, God, she prayed silently, *let him come to me at Christmas time.*

On the way back to the hospital, Bill couldn't see the traffic signals for the tears in his eyes.

What's the matter with me? I've never done this before. No one ever affected me in such a way. I just can't live without Alex.

It was a new experience for him, but then Bill Brant had never been in love before.

CHAPTER 11

Dr. Ken spent Thanksgiving with Caroline and her family at the Wells mansion on Squirrel Hill. The table was a vision of loveliness, as usual, and nothing was spared to serve Ken a delicious meal. He ate and relished it as he had no other Thanksgiving dinner.

Dr. John was able to go to the table and eat in his quaint dining room at Thirty-Second Street. He had invited some close friends, retired doctors and their wives, to enjoy the holiday with him, wondering if this would be his last time with his friends.

Bill Brant had to work at the hospital Thanksgiving Day, but he ate the traditional turkey and stuffing in the hospital cafeteria. He missed Alex Ann beyond belief and was looking forward, more than ever, to his trip at Christmas. He had already made reservations for a plane from Pittsburgh to Tampa. If nothing came up, it was better to have reservations and cancel them than not be able to get a seat at the last minute.

While he ate, he tried to visualize the Shaw family—what kind of home they had. Would they have friends in, or celebrate Thanksgiving alone, just the three of them?

It was cold in Pittsburgh, with about three inches of snow on the ground. Was it sunny and warm in Tampa? Was Alex responding to treatment as well as she had in Pittsburgh? Was she faithful in her exercises when there was no one around to prod her along? These and many more questions needed answers, and Bill Brant stood it as long as he could. Then he dialed the residence of Sam Shaw.

Much to his surprise, Alex answered the telephone. They had talked before by phone, but it was expensive and Bill had to watch his finances.

"Alex?" he questioned, shyly.

"Yes, Bill," she replied, happily.

"You knew my voice," he stated, slightly surprised.

"Of course. How could I mistake the voice of the one I love the most?" she teased.

"How's everything?"

"Fine, so far. My treatments are going along great. They don't have the equipment here that they have at West End, but this is a smaller hospital," she explained.

"Are you getting stronger?"

"It's hard to tell," she answered. "The therapist thinks I am, but I get tired so easily."

"That's understandable. As time goes on, you'll get stronger, and the fatigue will pass. Can you stand by yourself?"

"Not yet," she admitted. "Do you think I will soon? Oh, that will be such a glorious day! I can't wait! If I could stand alone, it wouldn't be hard to walk then, would it?"

"Now, don't get ahead of yourself," Bill cautioned. "You'll need a walker for a little while before you'll be able to walk by yourself. It will all fall into place if you have patience and endurance," he assured her.

"Let's not talk about me any more. How are things with you?" she asked.

"Lonely," Bill sighed. "I miss you something awful. It seems ages since I've held you. I keep busy so that time will pass quicker. Say a prayer that I'll be able to make the trip to Tampa for Christmas."

"I will," she replied fervently. "I'll say one every morning and evening, when I get up and when I go to bed. I have faith that your plans will all work out. They must, darling. I can't wait to see you," Alex cried excitedly.

"I love you," Bill said, "and would like to talk all evening, but I must hang up now. I'll call again next week. If you need me, make a person-to-person call to the hospital and they'll page me," he instructed. "Good night, my love, and keep working."

Alex Ann felt a terrible void after she replaced the receiver.

Why do people have to be separated when they love and need each other so much? Maybe I should have stayed in Pittsburgh. Her thoughts wandered from one problem to another. *Is it better here, or would it have been better there?*

"Who was that on the telephone, Alexandria?" Mervice inquired.

"It was Bill, Mother. He was lonely and called to see how I was. He has his reservations made for the Christmas holidays. Oh, Mother, I want so much to be able to stand with a walker when he comes," Alex Ann said wistfully. "I'm going to ask Dr. Wallace to let me try a walker next week, when I go for my treatment. Bill says I'll need a walker for a while, then crutches, until I'm strong enough to walk alone."

"Well, it will be wonderful when you can use a walker," Mervice agreed. "Getting around the house will be much easier. However, I want you to promise that you'll do it only if the doctors advise it. Promise me, Alexandria," her mother commanded.

"I promise, Mother," Alex agreed reluctantly. "I'll not do anything to make my condition worse...knowingly, that is. I'm anxious to get well, but I know I must crawl before I walk," she quipped.

Alexandria immediately began to plan for the Christmas holiday. She thought about the gifts she would purchase for Bill, and wondered what he would give her for their first Christmas together. The trip to Florida would be enough; he wouldn't have to buy her anything. Being with him was all she wanted.

The days continued to pass for Ken, Caroline, Bill and Alex Ann. Time also went on for Dr. John.

He realized that with each passing day he was becoming weaker and weaker. Soon the pain would return, and he would need sedatives all the time. Drugs had a way of wearing off, patients became addicted to them, and finally the suffering was unbearable. Dr. John hoped that wouldn't happen to him. He wished to just sleep away and not cause anyone further problems.

Dr. Minard wanted to give Caroline an engagement ring for Christmas. It was an important purchase for him, for he was going to ask Caroline to marry him. He wanted everything to be just right. Yet, if he so much as hinted it to her, she would guess what he was doing, and that would spoil everything.

He decided to work through his nurse to find out which type of ring Caroline would prefer—gold or platinum. Mary Ann could question Caroline and she wouldn't suspect anything. Mary Ann was the most efficient nurse-technician Ken had ever met, always able to contemplate his every move. She was always one step ahead of him and never ran out of energy.

"Her husband must have a screw loose, Ken decided. *How could he leave her with two small children? Mary Ann is everything a man could want in a wife.*

He had never talked with Mary Ann about her private life, and wondered if Caroline had. Maybe she knew the circumstances. He decided to ask Caroline about it.

"Caroline, have you ever talked with Mary Ann about her private life?" Ken asked her boldly.

"Yes," Caroline nodded. "She's had a pretty rough time since her husband was killed."

"Killed?" Ken cried. "How was he killed? I thought he left her." *That's how wrong one can be for jumping to conclusions,* he thought guiltily.

"He was in an automobile accident," Caroline revealed. "Killed instantly. She was left with those two small children to raise, which hasn't been easy. She's thankful for this job, which she really enjoys, but I think you've already surmised that."

"She seems quite well adjusted to her grief," Ken noted.

"Well...he's been dead for several years," Caroline said. "Mary Ellen was just fourteen months old when the accident happened, and she's five now. Roy, Jr. is in the second grade. Boy, it must be rough to raise children all alone in this day and age She doesn't appear to be bitter, though, or at least she doesn't let it show," Caroline admitted.

The patients began coming in again, two at a time, so Ken and Caroline were forced to discontinue their talk until later.

Ken's entire attitude toward Mary Ann changed from then on. He was forever playing Cupid, determined to marry her off to a rich doctor, but only if she promised to stay on as his assistant.

Mary Ann promised to stay on as long as he needed her, unless the children needed her more. She had some income from insurance and investments, but had to supplement it by working. She had hoped someday to quit working and have a home with a husband like other normal families. Until that day came, she was determined to make the best of it.

A couple of days later, Caroline ran into the office breathlessly.

"Let's have a party!" she cried.

"A party?" Ken questioned. "For whom? When? Where?"

"Here, for Dr. John, for his seventy-fifth birthday," Caroline explained excitedly.

"When is his birthday?" Mary Ann asked.

"The twenty-eighth of December. It might be his last one, and I thought it would be nice if we had a party for him. Please, Ken?" she pleaded.

"He's not very well, Caroline," Ken answered, feeling bad about having to dampen her enthusiasm. "Are you sure you know what you're doing?"

"I think a small party would be all right," she said. "We could invite just his closest friends, their wives, Dr. Brant, Mary Ann, you and me and, of course, Quinter. We could have it from seven-thirty until nine o'clock. That's only ninety minutes. That wouldn't be too much for him, would it?"

"Probably not, but we'll have to tell him. I don't think a surprise party would be a good idea. If he's not up to it, then no party, okay?" he instructed

"Okay," Caroline agreed, looking dejected.

She thought her idea was such a good one, but she realized then that she hadn't thought it through. What if they had a party and Dr. John got worse? Well, she was going to at least ask him, and she promised to abide by whatever he said.

Dr. John didn't get up very early, so she waited until lunch to approach him with her plan. She and Mary Ann would fix the refreshments so Quinter would be free to do other things:

decorating, cleaning and getting Dr. John ready for his big evening.

She didn't have much time to prepare for the party, with all the excitement of Christmas and the New Year, but she was determined to squeeze it in.

At noon, Caroline went bouncing up the stairs to the second floor suite in search of Dr. Blanding. She rang the bell.

"Come in," Quinter called.

Caroline opened the door and stuck her head in.

"Oh, it's you, Miss Wells. What a pleasant surprise," Quinter smiled.

"May I see Dr. John this afternoon?" she asked. "If he's sleeping, I don't want to bother him."

"He's not sleeping, and he'll be elated to see you," Quinter replied. "Please, go into his sitting room."

"Good afternoon, sir," Caroline said, approaching Dr. John. "I hope I'm not intruding. Quinter told me to come right in."

"Come in, Miss Wells," Dr. John urged. "How nice of you to come and visit a sick, old man."

"I didn't intend to disturb you, but I need your permission to do something. That gave me the courage to come," Caroline explained.

"What is it that I can do for you, Miss Wells?"

"First of all, call me Caroline," she instructed. "Miss Wells is too formal."

"All right, Caroline, what is it?" he smiled.

"Your birthday is just a few days after Christmas," she began. "We'd like to give you a small party—just about ten or twelve of your friends, along with the office staff and Ken. Do you feel up to a party so soon after Christmas?" she asked.

"Well," Dr. John said slowly, "Christmas won't be much different from any other day. Of course, I must insist that there be no presents," he stated firmly.

"Yes, we could arrange that," Caroline nodded her head vigorously. "Are you sure we wouldn't be imposing?"

"Not at all. I think it might be fun to have a birthday party. Seventy-five years...my, my, that's a long time to live," he said dreamily.

"Yes, sir, it is a long time, especially when you're looking forward," Caroline agreed. "Not so long, I suppose, when you look backward. We would like to invite some of your close friends. Mary Ann and I will bake a cake and bring the other refreshments. Will you tell me who you'd like to invite?"

"I'll give you a list of the couples I would like, and you bring whomever you please," he replied. "Thank you, Caroline, for thinking of me. I'll never forget your kindness."

"We'll talk more later. Now, I must get back to work," Caroline said. "Good-bye for now."

"What did he say?" Ken asked, when Caroline bounced back into the office.

"He was very pleased," she exclaimed. "He said he would give me a list of guests and that I was to bring whomever I wanted. Isn't that great!" she cried.

"You could cheer up a mad hatter!" Ken laughed. "Where do you get all your energy and brilliant ideas?"

"Good blood, doctor, good blood," she giggled in that devilish laugh that was so tantalizing.

Ken and Caroline went to the church service at eleven o'clock on Christmas Eve. It was a first for Ken, because the Tampa church hadn't had a service on Christmas Eve.

Caroline sang the soprano solos in the cantata, "Night of Miracles." Ken occupied the back pew, as usual, just in case he was called out.

The choir lined up in the narthex of the church, and an organ prelude began. The congregation stood, and at exactly eleven o'clock the trumpeter stepped into the aisle and led the choir to the loft, singing, "O Come, All Ye Faithful."

When the choir was in place, Reverend Stoddard stepped behind the pulpit and gave the invocation. The choir and congregation were then seated. Reverend Stoddard read the traditional Christmas Story from the Gospel of Luke, then said the evening prayer.

After singing of the cantata, a candlelighting service was held. The ushers went forward and lighted four candles from the main altar candle, then, slowly proceeding back along the church aisle, they lit the candles at the end of each pew. Each parishioner lit his small candle from a neighbor's candle, until the entire church was glowing. The church lights were turned off. They sang "Silent Night," put their offerings in the plate in the narthex, and quietly left the church.

After they were in the car, Ken remarked, "I've never been to a service to compare with that one. I thought my baptism, by triune immersion, was a moving service, but this one left me breathless. Your solos were perfect. That was really a beautiful cantata."

"Thank you, darling," Caroline whispered. "I'm so happy that we belong to the same church and that we enjoy going to church. It makes Christmas so meaningful."

When they arrived at the Wells' mansion, Caroline's parents had not yet arrived. It was the opportunity for which Ken had been waiting.

He had purchased a large, heart-shaped engagement ring with one large diamond in the center, set in yellow gold, with three smaller diamonds around it. He hoped to have enough time to present it to Caroline before her parents arrived.

"Would you like a cup of coffee, Ken?" Caroline offered.

"No, thank you," he replied. "It's too late for me to drink coffee. Come and sit beside me. I want to see what it's like to be with you for our first Christmas Eve," he announced.

Caroline approached the settee and sat close to Ken. He took a small box from his coat pocket and handed it to her.

"I want to give you this tonight," he said in a husky whisper. "I'll be busy in the morning for a while, and may not see you until noon," he explained.

Carefully, Caroline undid the wrapping on the box, opened the lid, and cried when she saw what was inside.

"Oh, Darling!" she exclaimed. "How beautiful! I never expected to receive such a gift!" She removed the ring from the box and handed it to Ken. "Will you put it on?"

As Ken took the ring from her outstretched hand, and put it on the third finger of her left hand, he said, "Will you marry me?"

"Yes...oh, yes," she cried. "When? When do you want to marry me?"

"As soon as possible," he replied. "I know it will take time to make plans, and Dr. John...we'll need to consider his condition, too. But I want you as quickly as we can arrange it."

"I'm so happy I could shout," Caroline smiled. "What will Mother and Dad say?"

"Do you think they'll object?" Ken asked, suddenly worried. "Are you sure you can live on a doctor's salary? I won't be able to give you all the nice things you've been accustomed to."

"Do you think my parents will object? I don't think so. Yes, my darling, I can live on a doctor's salary as long as the doctor is you," Caroline answered. "Just love me always. That's all I ask."

"That's easy, but will you love me always, Caroline?"

"Always...doctor...always," Caroline whispered.

At that moment, Caroline's parents came in.

"What's all the commotion?" her father asked.

"We have just become engaged," Caroline announced happily. "And, oh, Daddy, I'm so happy. Say you're happy, too!"

"I'm happy, sweetheart," he reassured her. "Congratulations, Ken," he said, reaching out a hand to shake with Ken. "It'll be hard to give her up, but we knew it was inevitable."

Caroline's mother was hugging her daughter. She kissed Ken's cheek, then said, "Welcome to our family, Doctor. I guess you're the one for Caroline. I've never seen her so happy."

"Thank you for wanting me as a member of your family," Ken replied graciously. "We'll be married as soon as we can, but there are many things to consider before we set the date." Ken glanced at his wristwatch. "It's late now, and I think I should be going home and letting you folks go to bed. I'll have to make rounds at the hospital in the morning."

"You'll be here for Christmas dinner, won't you?" Caroline asked anxiously.

"Yes, I plan to be here if I have no emergencies. Thank you for inviting me."

Caroline walked with Ken to the door.

"Oh, Ken, I'm so ecstatic!" she cried. "I won't be able to sleep a wink!"

Their arms went around each other, and they wished the moment could last forever. Then Ken was gone.

Caroline was a bit surprised that her mother was so anxious for their happiness. She had been against Caroline's relationship with Ken Minard, until she met Ken at church. After that, she changed her attitude.

He is a good doctor, she thought, *or so the Medical Society tells me, so he'll probably make more money after he gets well established. Caroline's so happy, and that's all that matters.*

She was still reluctant to let her "baby" go, perhaps because she was their only child. Boys were inclined to leave home and be overly independent. Girls always needed their mothers, especially at the birth of their babies.

Christine was elated at the thought of having grandchildren. They next day was Christmas. Christine wondered what it would be like to have grandchildren around on Christmas. It would be like reliving the joys and sorrows they'd had with Caroline.

Christmas...the most festive holiday of the year, and the most religious time of the year. It passed so quickly and was gone until another year. Christine and Roy Wells tried to observe the Christmas spirit all through the year. Christine hoped her daughter and Ken would also live the same life. If he was a good doctor, he certainly would practice goodwill all year.

Dr. Brant boarded the plane at two-forty p.m., at the Greater Pittsburgh Airport for his trip to Tampa, Florida, to spend Christmas with Alex Ann and her family. The trip was smooth and fast. Before Bill realized it, the stewardess was announcing that passengers should fasten their seat belts for the approach to Tampa.

Bill traveled light, for he expected to be there only a short time. He would have to return to Pittsburgh the day after Christmas. Another therapist was standing in for him for the short time he would be away. Christmas Day was usually quiet at the hospital, unless an unexpected emergency came up.

The plane landed at Tampa Airport at five p.m., taxied into the terminal and Bill alighted. He started through the long tunnel that led from the plane to the waiting rooms for passengers loading and unloading. He took the shuttle car from the plane to the main terminal building and to his surprise he saw a girl with a walker coming toward him.

"Alex!" he shouted. "Alex Ann! You're using a walker. I'm so proud of you!" He hugged her to him for a minute.

"Welcome to Tampa, Darling," she murmured. "I wanted to surprise you, so I've practiced all week."

"That's the best Christmas present I could have had," he said fervently. He turned to Mr. and Mrs. Shaw. "Isn't she something?" he crowed proudly. "So beautiful, and now she can walk with a walker. I can't believe it!"

"Welcome to Tampa, Dr. Brant," Sam Shaw said, grabbing Bill's hand and shaking it so hard that Bill winced.

Bill hugged Mervice Shaw and she welcomed him with a kiss on the cheek.

"We need to pick up your bags and get Alexandria back to her wheelchair so she doesn't overdo herself," Mervice explained. "This is the first time she's been away from home and I don't want her to get exhausted."

"Right away," Bill stated. "I have only a small grip with a few clothes and a couple of presents. Be with you in a few minutes." Bill took off on a run toward the baggage wheel.

Within a few minutes, they were in the car and headed across town to the Shaw home.

"I want to spend the evening and tomorrow with you and my parents," Alex Ann announced. "I have invited some of my friends in tomorrow evening so they can meet you and learn to love you, as we all do," she bragged.

"Great, but I just want to be with you," Bill said. "I don't care if there's anyone else there or not."

He marveled at how he could board a plane in Pittsburgh and in less than three hours to be in the tropical city of Tampa, Florida—from snow to sunshine in one hundred and twenty minutes.

Sam was looking forward to showing Bill around the town. Maybe he would be able to steal him away after the big Christmas dinner. Alex Ann would need to rest for a while, and Mervice would supervise the maid in cleaning up.

Bill Brant was not the type of man that Sam would have chosen for his daughter to spend the rest of her life with, but when he saw how she had changed and how happy she was, he had to admit she knew what she was doing. The only important thing was that Alex would walk again, drive a car and dance as she did before. It would take a long time for everything to come about, but Alex's morale was as important as anything in the fight to survive. Bill Brant was her greatest ally in that field.

The traffic was hectic in Tampa on the day before Christmas, and it took the entourage longer than usual to get across town.

"It sure is easier to fly all the way from Pittsburgh to Tampa than to drive through this traffic," Bill noted.

Many of the winter guests and tourists had arrived, and more would arrive after Christmas. Also, the Florida folks had relatives who spent Christmas with them. It created quite a stampede at times.

"It's wonderful that older folks have the opportunity to come to a warmer climate during the winter," Bill observed. "It's much easier on them."

"That's true," Sam agreed. "Tomorrow, we'll take a drive around to see the bay and some of the other attractions in Tampa."

Alex sighed with relief and relaxed in the back seat, thankful to be alive and as well as she was. She was also grateful to have Bill with her. All was peace and good will for this Christmas season.

CHAPTER 12

Spring came early to Pittsburgh and likewise to Tampa. Alex Ann had progressed to being able to walk with the aid of a cane. She vowed that on her wedding day she would throw away the cane and walk down the aisle on her father's arm.

I'm going to be married, she thought with awe. *I can't believe it. I've been crippled for so long, and now I can walk, almost without limping. If I practice, I'm sure I'll be able to get down the bridal path with Daddy's assistance.*

Alex Ann planned in her mind, and on paper, all the things she wanted to do that day. Her day... for after all, wasn't the bride the center of attraction at any wedding? Everyone would be looking at her, not the groom nor the elaborately-dressed women who attended, but right at her. It made Alex feel so important. There would never be another day in her life when all eyes would be on her as they would on her wedding day.

Bill had been transferred to a Tampa hospital to be near Alex, and instruct her in the therapy at home as well as the rigorous workout at the hospital twice a week. She was making excellent progress.

It was spring and everyone felt a new beginning at that time of the year. Bill missed his friends in Pittsburgh, but was elated with the beautiful warm Florida days and cool night of the tropical setting, and of the chance to be with Alex.

Their wedding was only a week away, and Ken and Caroline were invited. Bill hadn't told Alex, for he wanted it to be a surprise. It would have been nice for Caroline to be in the bridal party, so he intended to work that out with his future mother-in-law. Bill had asked Ken to be his best man, which would be another surprise for Alex. All he'd told her was that a doctor friend of his was coming from Pittsburgh to be his best man. He mentioned no friends.

Ken was reluctant at first, what with having to leave Dr. John, who needed him most. Bill suggested that since Dr. John was in bed most of the time, maybe Ken could instruct Quinter in his care, and they could leave Tampa for Pittsburgh as soon as the reception was over and they could secure a flight.

Bill and Alex would have to postpone having a honeymoon. Bill was just becoming established in Tampa, and they would be moving into a new apartment on the seventh floor of a condominium facing the ocean front. The view was breathtaking, and the red and gold sunsets in Florida were beyond description.

Bill wished he'd studied painting just so he could capture some of the incomparable beauty on canvas. He missed the mountains of Pennsylvania, but was willing to give up everything to be married to Alex. They planned to go back each summer and spend their vacation roaming the hills and valleys of Ligonier Valley.

Daydream time was over for Bill. His next patient was wheeled in and his psychology as well as his physical abilities were on trial once more.

Ken leafed through his mail and discovered the announcement and invitation to Alex Ann Shaw's wedding. The gold and white announcement read:

Mr. and Mrs. Samuel Shaw

request your presence at the marriage

of their daughter

Alexandria Ann Shaw

to

Dr. William Lee Brant

to be held in the garden of the Shaw Home

21 Belding Place, Tampa, Florida

on April twenty-two, at two-thirty p.m.

Reception following at:

Green Bay Country Club

Alex Ann was going to be married. Ken found it hard to believe. And to think there was a time when he thought he would marry Alex. He now knew that he hadn't known then what real love was. It was only after he met Caroline and learned to love her that he found he'd never loved Alex...romantically, that is. She was a good friend, and he hoped that she, as well as her new husband, would continue to be his friends.

Ken didn't feel free to accept Bill's invitation to be his best man because of Dr. John's condition. The old doctor was in bed most of the time. He had lived longer than anticipated, and it was quite a chore for Quinter to care for him night and day. He had a nurse for one shift of the day, so Quinter could rest.

Ken looked after Dr. John on Quinter's day off and the shift that the nurse was off. If Ken could get someone to help out during those times, he would be glad to be best man at Bill's wedding.

The only thing to do was ask Dr. John how he felt about Ken's leaving. He was sure the old man would want him to go, but Ken would feel guilty about leaving unless he had someone to help.

"I received an invitation to Alex Ann's wedding, and her mother has asked me to be a bridesmaid," Caroline announced. "It's on the Q.T., though; she doesn't want Alex to know. Do you think I should accept?"

"That's up to you," Ken replied. "I received an invitation, too, and Bill wants me to be best man, also on the Q.T."

"We'll need to answer the invitation by tomorrow, so I'll get things lined up today, if possible, and call Bill this evening or tomorrow morning," Ken went on.

"Oh, I want to go so badly," Caroline sighed, "but I wish it was our wedding. I will have to be satisfied until later, I know, but it's so hard to wait when I love you so much."

"Our day will come, Darling. In the meantime, I'll discuss my plans with Quinter and Dr. John and see if I can work out something," Ken decided.

"Mother said she felt I should go and is willing to pay my fare," Caroline revealed. "She was hoping you'd be able to go with me. She doesn't want to see her 'little girl' go off on a trip all by herself," Caroline giggled. "I tried to convince her that I'm fully capable of taking care of myself, but you know how mothers are."

That same evening, while Ken was helping with Dr. John, he approached him with the plan.

"I'll only do it if you feel free to let me go," Ken asserted, "and if you're certain that Quinter and Mrs. Neal can manage without me."

"Yes, of course, Ken, you must go," Dr. John urged. "Mrs. Neal said that her husband would help out any time we needed him, and I'm sure I'll be all right with the two of them. When will you go? Who'll take over while you're gone?" Dr. John inquired.

"We'll leave Friday afternoon, and return Sunday," Ken explained. "That's the first flight back that's available after the wedding and reception."

"It sounds splendid to me," Dr. John affirmed. "You must go, or Alexandria will be so disappointed when she finds out you were to be the best man and didn't come."

"All right," Ken agreed, a little reluctantly, "we'll go ahead and make our plans to leave Friday. I'll have Dr. Zell stand by for me, if he will, and we'll close the office all day Friday. I'll need to call Loi, my houseboy, and tell him we're coming. We'll stay there until rehearsal time, since Alex isn't to know about this until the last possible minute."

"Fine, I hope your plans work out," Dr. John smiled.

Dr. John felt sad after Ken left. He wanted to attend the wedding, but knew his time for such things was past. He didn't feel bitter, for he'd had his season in life. It was somebody else's turn.

The reservations were made. Ken made arrangements with Dr. Zell to take over his emergencies, and Mr. Neal agreed to help with Dr. John. Ken was beginning to get excited, not only about the wedding, but about returning home.

How would it feel to be home? Warm weather...sunshine...perhaps some water skiing and a little swimming. He would have to wait and see how everything worked out.

"I must call Bill and tell him we'll be there," Ken muttered.

"What are you mumbling about?" Mary Ann demanded.

"Our plans for the wedding, they're all set," Ken explained. "I just pray that they work out."

"You'll do fine," Mary Ann reassured him. "Just think positively. It'll be nice to have an extra day off next week. Three days in a row...my, my, how will we all stand it?" she teased.

Imagine life being that simple, Ken thought. *Just think positively and it will happen. Well, it helps, anyway,* he decided.

Caroline was in a dither, wondering about what she would wear to the wedding. She would need a new dress, and wanted it to be blue. She would have to take a day off from work, which would cause problems at the office, but there was no recourse.

Caroline and Christine went to the two largest department stores that featured bridal wear. Caroline tried on dress after dress, then finally chose a blue organza with a high, Empire waistline. Her slim figure was her greatest asset, and she resembled a New York model.

Since the bridesmaids weren't wearing matching gowns, this made it easier for Caroline to choose her dress. There would be five bridesmaids and the Maid of Honor.

"Gee, I don't know any of the other girls," Caroline complained, "and Alex thinks she's having only five attendants. I hate to surprise her like this, but her mother insisted." Caroline was so excited that she wondered how she was able to choose the right accessories.

The attendants weren't wearing anything on their heads, so that eliminated a long hunt for the right headpiece. Caroline would need to have her hair done the morning of their departure.

So much to do...no time...no time...such confusion. Christine was anxious for the day of their departure to arrive.

"What if it rains the day of the wedding?" her mother asked. "Have they made other arrangements?"

"I'm sure they have," Caroline replied calmly. "Isn't this exciting?"

Christine could see that her daughter's own wedding was going to be a lot of work and worry. She hoped they would be able to hang onto their daughter for a while. She was sure it wouldn't be long before she would be going through the same things that Mervice Shaw was now encountering.

The big day finally arrived. Ken and Caroline were off to Florida to attend the wedding. The fact that the plane was thirty minutes late left Ken "chomping at the bit," until finally they were aboard and on their way.

Ken's luggage was minute in comparison with Caroline's. Bill was renting Ken a formal suit, so he wouldn't have to transport that all the way down.

Caroline's gown proved to be a bit of a problem. She put it in a plastic bag and had Ken carry it onto the plane, so it would be ready to wear the next day. Everything had to be done beforehand, for they wouldn't have a minute to spare.

As the plane sped toward Tampa, the captain announced that they were going over the Shenandoah Valley of Virginia at 37,000 feet. Caroline's eyes were glued to the beautiful scenery below. When Ken spoke, it startled her.

"Maybe when we're married, we can drive through that beautiful countryside instead of flying so far above it," he suggested. "It really is one of the most breathtaking scenes in all of the United States."

"It must be. I've never seen anything to compare with it," Caroline admitted, "but then I haven't traveled that much, either. Maybe we could take a trip each year. Can you do things like that on a doctor's salary?" she asked, jokingly.

"Let's hope so." He laughed.

At that moment, the captain spoke again. They were entering a turbulence area, and he asked that all seat belts be secured. Caroline didn't enjoy this part of the airplane ride, but the big plane was going so fast that they would be through the storm in a short time.

"We are approaching Tampa airport," the captain announced a while later. "It will be a little rough on descent, so please, fasten all seat belts."

The trip had gone so fast and they were already at their destinations. Caroline couldn't believe it. The big jet taxied into the terminal and they passed through the tunnel to the waiting room, picked up their luggage and took the shuttle car to the main terminal.

"I wonder where Loi is," Ken mused. "I thought he would be here in the waiting room to meet us. Surely he understood my instructions."

"He's probably in the terminal," Caroline suggested. "Have patience, Dr. Minard," she teased.

Loi was waiting in the main terminal, and Ken introduced Caroline to him. The luggage was divided up and they headed for the parking area.

"I was beginning to think you hadn't come," Ken admitted to Loi.

"Oh, yes, sir, Mr. Ken, I come, but I not ride that fancy car to waiting room. It throw everybody around. I scared," Loi muttered.

"There's nothing to it. When we return, you can go over with Caroline and me, and you won't be afraid," Ken suggested. "Once you ride it, you will do so at every opportunity."

Home...after so many months. Ken found it really wasn't home anymore. He lived in Pittsburgh now, where he'd taken on a heavy task, but a glorious one. Pittsburgh was home to him now, and probably would be until he retired.

The weather was exceptional for April. The days would be sunny and the nights balmy. Where on earth was there weather to compare with it? It was still cold in Pittsburgh.

"It's so clean here," Caroline noted, on the way to the cottage. "It looks like everything was scrubbed and polished just for our arrival."

"Tampa doesn't have the industry that Pittsburgh has, and the city doesn't get as dirty," Ken explained. "Then it rains more often here and that bathes and cleanses the scenery. Have you ever been to Florida before?"

"Once, when I was about seven, but that's so long ago. We went to Miami, and I think I grew up feeling Miami was Florida. You see, when we vacationed, it was to the mountains or the Jersey shore. Daddy's not much for beaches. He'd rather go to the cool forests and swim in the mountain lakes. We've visited many state forest parks. It was such fun. However, I'm looking forward to our stay here, even though it will be short," she said enthusiastically.

"Here we are," Ken announced.

"It's beautiful!" Caroline exclaimed. "Real Florida living!"

It was almost six p.m., and the rehearsal was at seven-thirty. They would have no time for a swim or a walk on the beach until the following day.

Ken's seashore home was small in comparison to the average home. Everything was on one floor: three bedrooms, a vast living room and dinette, and a thirty-foot family room with double glass doors that opened onto a screened porch. From the porch, one could look out onto the bay and see water...miles of it. It seemed endless. The walk-in kitchen was also off the screened porch and there was a pass-through from it to the porch.

Caroline's bedroom opened onto a concrete deck that housed a twenty-four-foot swimming pool and screen enclosure.

"How wonderful!" she cried. "It's all so gorgeous. I can't believe I'm really here!"

Ken's bedroom opened onto the same lanai, and in a few seconds he was in his bathing suit and had dived into the pool. Caroline couldn't swim because her hair had been done for the wedding. However, she intended to make up for lost time after the wedding was over.

The wedding rehearsal was a problem for Alex Ann. Her legs were not strong enough, so she needed her cane for the evening rehearsal. She was determined to put it aside for the wedding the next day.

The organ began, the soloist practiced, and then it was time for Alex to rehearse her wedding vows with Bill.

Bill was there, and knew Ken and Caroline would be entering soon. He smiled as he thought how surprised Alex would be when she saw them.

Sam and Alex practiced walking up the aisle, then the rehearsal began. There was a chair at the altar so Alex could be seated during the remainder of the rehearsal.

When the groom and best man appeared, Alex cried, "Ken Minard! Bill, you didn't tell me you asked Ken to be your best man."

"I wanted to surprise you, so I had to tell a little white lie," Bill laughed.

The Matron of Honor, chosen by Alex, was up front, and the Flower Girl was about half way down the bridal path to the altar. At that moment, Caroline started down the aisle.

"Caroline!" Alex shouted. "How did you work this out without me knowing?" she demanded. "Oh, I'm so happy, I'm going to cry!"

The rehearsal stopped momentarily, until Alex's eyes were dried. The surprise was over and they could get down to the business of who stood where. Thus, the evening passed.

The rehearsal was followed by a reception dinner.

"I'm so nervous I can hardly stand it," Alex remarked. "I can't wait until I'm Bill's wife, and I'm so pleased you and Ken could be here," she said to Caroline. "Thank you, Mother, for your schemes and elegant plans behind my back. You really are precious."

April 22nd dawned sunny and clear. The weatherman promised there would be no rain, so everything was perfect. The gazebo had been erected; the flowers would be placed on either side of the kneeling bench later in the afternoon. The day promised to be perfect in every way.

The men in the bridal party carried a portable organ into the gazebo. The soloist was deciding where she would stand. Caroline and Ken had arrived to join in the excitement, but Mervice Shaw was sad.

I don't know why I'm sad, she thought. *Alexandria and Bill love each other, and she can walk now with a little help. This should be the happiest day of my life.*

Mervice Shaw was giving up a part of herself...her only daughter. The tears welled up in her eyes, as she continued with her work, until the view was completely obliterated. She wiped at the drops.

"Don't cry, Mother," Alex begged. "I'm not going away. Not very far, that is. I'll see you often. Please be happy for me."

"I am happy for you, Alex, but it's hard to give up someone so precious in your life, even if it is only to her new husband. You've been through so much and I want you to be happy, but you are my only child and my baby. Mothers always feel that way. I'm sorry; I'll try to be brave."

"How I envy you," Caroline said, while she dashed around helping to place the kneeling bench and flower stands. She had volunteered to do these things so Alex could rest as much as possible before the big event. "I wish it was my wedding. I know my turn will come, and I'm so happy for you and Bill, but I'm also anxious to have my own wedding and start married life."

"When do you and Ken plan to be married?" Alex asked.

"It depends on Dr. John. He's in bed most of the time now. He's failed so much in the past weeks. I'm afraid he won't live much longer. Ken helps take care of him, and we can't get married as long as he's doing that. We could have a small ceremony, but, like you, I want a big wedding and a reception at the Country Club. Do you think I'm being selfish?" Caroline went on working as she spoke.

"Of course not," Mervice interjected. "All girls dream of a fine wedding, and you'll be glad for the rest of your life that you waited until the right time to be married."

"Dr. John is a wonderful person," Alex sighed. "It's sad that his life is over, but I know he wouldn't want me to be sad today no matter how he feels."

At that moment, the telephone rang, and Caroline dashed to answer it. The maid announced that it was for Alexandria. Alex took her cane and hurried as fast as she could to the telephone.

"All happiness to you, Alexandria, and to Bill, too." Dr. John Blanding was on the other end of the wire.

"Oh, thank you, Dr. John," Alex Ann replied, ecstatic. "How nice of you to call me on my wedding day. Are you all right?" she asked suddenly.

"I'm as well as I can be," he assured her. "Did the folks get there all right?"

"Yes, Ken and Caroline are here, and I was so surprised that I cried," Alex admitted. "That made my wedding perfect. The weather is beautiful today, and I'm so happy that I'll be able to walk the bridal path without my cane. I'm going to lean on Daddy."

"That is good news, Alex," Dr. John said. "It makes me feel good not only that you're to be married, but you have made so much progress otherwise." He sighed, as though the talking was taking a great deal of effort. "I'll say a few words to Bill, if he's there, and bless you, Alexandria Shaw—soon-to-be-Brant—in all you do. Please, take care of yourself."

"Oh, I will, Dr. John, and you do the same." She knew it would be the last time she'd hear Dr. John's voice, which sounded so weak. She forced herself to become interested in other things and not dwell on the illness of Dr. John.

For a moment, she wondered what it was going to be like, married to a doctor. Would he discuss his patients with her? Would she be able to help him in his practice? She would have some adjusting to do, and hoped she would have the strength to do it.

CHAPTER 13

Everything was in its place. The wedding guests were arriving four and six at a time. Alexandria was dressed, except for the veil.

Her wedding gown was an off-white lace, with fitted bodice, long sleeves, a stand-up collar and a long train. She had chosen a long veil, held in place by a crown of seed pearls and small rhinestones. She wore fabric-made pumps in the same shade as the dress, and carried a spray of yellow and white roses—her favorite flowers.

It was time to begin. Now, it seemed that time had passed so quickly. Had she done everything she wanted to do as a single girl? Would she regret being married? Would it be hard to leave home? Would she miss her little-girl life? She was grown up now, and had gone through so much. Would her legs hold up through the ceremony? They had shortened her dress slightly for that reason. Visions flashed through her mind as the soloist began to sing.

Alex and her father walked to the head of the bridal path. A chair was placed there so Alex could sit down until it was time for the Bridal March.

The bridegroom and best man were in place, and the Maid of Honor had started down the aisle. She was followed by the flower girl—a four-year-old daughter of a friend. Susan was a beautiful, feminine child, and she performed perfectly. The audience stood, and when they glimpsed Susan, a murmur rustled through the crowd. The other bridesmaids started down the aisle.

Caroline was excited. She caught sight of Ken, and her eyes were transfixed on him as she walked down the aisle.

Will my wedding compare with this one? she wondered.

Then she was up front. She turned and faced the audience and the organ music swelled. The bridesmaids all stepped into place, and Alex took her place at the head of the bridal path with her father.

The organ music was all that could be heard. Alex Ann was so nervous, and her father tried to steady her.

Before they took the first step, he kissed her, and said, "Be happy, Alexandria, and brave. I'll help you all I can." They started off.

Bill Brant was "shivering in his shoes," the plight of all bridegrooms. When Alexandria came into sight, a smile burst forth from his face and he forgot his nervousness. He could see nothing but his exquisitely beautiful, radiant bride, who would be, in a few minutes, his wife.

In a fifteen-minute-ceremony, Alexandria Ann Shaw became Mrs. William Brant. The day had come, so slowly, and now it was going, all too soon, for both Alex and Bill. At that moment, they were the happiest couple in the world.

They left the gazebo to the strains of Mendelssohn's "Wedding March." The wedding party dispersed and made plans to go to the Country Club for the reception.

Ken and Caroline left the wedding reception about ten o'clock, and went back to Ken's home. They were both exhausted. After a short swim, they went to bed, knowing that the next day they would leave beautiful Florida for Pittsburgh and work once again.

Ken had rented a boat so they could go deep-sea fishing in the morning. He had used the *Ketter M* many times before, because it was equipped with a marine radio. Any messages Ken or Caroline received at the house could be relayed to them, through Loi and the telephone company.

They were up at six a.m., and on the Gulf of Mexico by seven. It was going to be a beautiful day, sunny, and probably quite hot, but the sea breeze would keep them from suffocating in the heat. "What if I get seasick?" Caroline asked. It was a first for her.

"You won't get seasick," Ken assured her. "The Gulf will be as calm as the bathtub today. The weather report is perfect. It's only when there are squalls and the sea is rough that one gets seasick. Besides, you're the advocate of 'think positive.'" He was stretching the truth a bit, but he didn't want Caroline to be frightened into becoming seasick.

They were about ten miles out into the Gulf when Caroline caught her first fish.

"This is the most exciting thing I've ever done!" she squealed. "Could we stay all day?"

"Most of it, but we do have a plane to catch," he reminded her. "This weather is just great. It's too bad we can't take some of the sunshine along. I suppose, though, that Pittsburgh will be hot enough this summer."

"Can we come back and spend a week fishing next time?" Caroline asked.

"Yes, on our honeymoon," Ken nodded. "Would you like a honeymoon on the sea?"

"You'd better believe it. I'd adore it, and most of all, I'd adore being married to you," Caroline gushed happily.

The time passed too quickly for the couple, and Caroline couldn't believe it when Ken anchored the boat and announced that it was lunch time.

"I'm hungry, too, Miss Wells," he stated. "What's to eat?"

"Some sandwiches, grapefruit sections, bananas, and soda," she replied. "What more would you like, Doctor? Oh, I forgot! There's the wedding cake. Alex gave us some to bring along today."

"Great. Just serve it up, please, Love."

They were just finishing their lunch when the radio caught Ken's attention.

"Calling the *Ketter M*. Calling the *Ketter M*. Do you read me *Ketter M*?"

Ken immediately recognized Loi's voice.

"That's Loi," Ken said. "Something must have happened. He wouldn't call unless there was an emergency." He reached over and grabbed the mike. "This is *Ketter M* ." Ken replied in a loud voice. "We read you loud and clear, Loi. What's happening?"

"There is telephone call from Pittsburgh," his houseboy replied in his usual broken English. "Dr. John worse. Want you come immediately."

"Message received," Ken replied. "We'll be there in a little while, Loi."

The anchor was lifted, and the two ate the balance of their lunch on the way into the marina.

"Now I understand why that radio is so important to you, Ken," Caroline said. "We wouldn't have known about Dr. John if it hadn't been for that radio."

"We may be too late, anyway," Ken said worriedly, his face solemn. "I'm afraid Dr. John will lapse into a coma before we can get to him. Then he wouldn't know that we were there with him. It's important that we get there as soon as possible."

It was impossible for them to get an earlier flight. They would have to take their original flight and hope for the best.

At five-thirty p.m., they were aboard their plane and speeding toward Pittsburgh. Ken had called the Shaw residence and told them the news of Dr. John.

"Tell Alex and Bill that we're sorry to have to leave so soon and on such short notice," he related. "We greatly enjoyed the festivities and thank you for inviting us. We'll pray for Alex's recover," he added.

Ken and Caroline went straight to the hospital from the airport. Dr. John was still conscious but failing fast.

"Dr. John." Ken bent over and wasted figure on the bed. "It's Ken. How are you doing?"

"I'm afraid the end is near," the old man replied in a weak voice. "Did I disturb your plans? I didn't mean to spoil your stay in Florida. Quinter was upset and insisted on calling you."

"You disturbed nothing, Doctor. I was happy to return so I could be here with you," Ken replied. "The wedding was beautiful and everything went off splendidly. The Shaw family sent their regards and prayers."

"I'm glad everything went well. I'm so tired...too tired to fight any longer. I'm perfectly ready...to pass onto a better place...knowing that you're here...and will carry on for me," Dr. John said in a halting voice.

"I could never fill your shoes, sir, nor could anyone else. I'll do my best, though, to live up to your expectations," Ken vowed. "I think you should rest now, and not talk any more."

At five minutes past four the next morning, Dr. John Blanding died. Ken and Caroline were by his side when his breathing was forever silent. He had lapsed into a coma about eleven-thirty the previous night, and died as peacefully as if he'd been sleeping.

The young couple walked silently away from the bedside of the great man who had given his all to his fellowman.

Caroline broke the silence with a choked statement, "It will be a big job to fill his shoes, Sweetheart. Do you think you can do it?"

"No, Darling, no one could ever replace Dr. John Blanding," Ken admitted truthfully. "He was one of a kind."

They went back to the office and home on Thirty-Second Street, where Caroline called her parents and told them that she was home safely and that Dr. John had passed away. When she hung up, she turned to the man she loved so much.

"What will you do now, Ken?" she asked softly.

"Well...you know that Dr. Blanding left me everything. I was all the family he had. Three weeks ago he told me he'd left me the house and all his holdings. He had a trust set up for the Crippled Children's Hospital, and one for Quinter. It's up to me to use or dispose of things as I see fit. What an awful job to have to dispose of a half century of someone's life!" Ken cried.

"Someone has to do it," Caroline said. "I'm just glad that he chose someone who cares so much for him, instead of it having to be a stranger. Was he wealthy?"

"Yes, very," Ken admitted, "and tomorrow or the next day I'll know just how much. Dr. John was rich in so many ways. Yet he must have been so lonely at times. It's too bad his wife couldn't have lived to share his joys as well as his disappointments," Ken lamented.

As he stood on the silent knoll of Forest Hill Cemetery, Ken wasn't thinking of the money and responsibility left to him by Dr. John. The words of the minister faded away to Ken's inner thoughts.

I have no one left; first Mother, then Father. When Mrs. Blanding died, I still had Dr. John, but now he is gone, too. Why didn't I have a brother or sister like other families? he wondered. *Where will I go for advice? Who will I confide in?*

The funeral was over. Friends were moving away from the grave, but Ken seemed rooted to the spot. Caroline touched him softly.

"Ken, come on," she urged. "Everyone is leaving. We must go home now."

"Home? I'm sorry, Caroline; my mind was far away. They're all gone now, I have no one left," he sobbed.

"You have me, Darling, for the rest of your life, if you want me," Caroline whispered.

Roy Wells noticed that Ken was in a state of near collapse, and left Christine's side to go to him.

"Come on, son, let's go home," he urged, his manner much softer than usual. "We're your family now. Dr. John wouldn't want you to grieve this way."

The office was closed for three days, but life had to go on, and Ken Minard still had a tremendous job to do.

Each patient, saddened by Dr. John's death, expressed his sympathy and expounded on how glad he was that Ken was there in his place.

"In his place! I could never take his place," Ken protested. "My very best is all I can do. I must remember that that's all that's required of me."

The first day back at work since Dr. John's death finally passed, and both Ken and Caroline were glad to close the office and go home.

"Come home with me, Ken," she urged. "It will be so lonely for you since Quinter is away."

Quinter had left immediately after the funeral for a much-needed vacation. He was terribly distressed over his old friend's death. He planned to return if Ken needed him; if not, Quinter would travel for a while, then settle in a community for retired folks. He was tired and deserved a rest.

"Okay," Ken agreed, "I'll change and be there at seven."

Dinner passed without incident. After coffee in the drawing room, Ken and Caroline went outside and walked the two blocks to the park on Squirrel Hill.

"It's beautiful here in the summer," Ken noted. "Cool and sunny. Maybe it won't get so hot this year." There was little emotion in his voice. Ken was quite dejected.

"What can I do to help?" Caroline pleaded. "How can I ease your pain?"

Ken turned and took her in his arms. "Love me," he whispered huskily, "just love me." He kissed her softly, and held her so tightly it was almost impossible for them to breathe.

"I do love you, and I always will," Caroline promised.

"Marry me, Caroline...right away," Ken begged. "Marry me, so I can be close to you all the time. I need you so much right now, and for always."

"Yes, Ken...right away," Caroline agreed without hesitation.

They were enclosed in each other's arms, and time ceased. The only thing that mattered at that moment was the two of them.